"You are the o
father possess
Xavier said with deceptive ~~~~~

Something deep inside curled into a tight, painful ball, and she wanted nothing more than to turn and walk from the room, the building…anything to escape the compelling man who held her father's fate in his hands.

"You're suggesting I become a form of human payment?" Each word took immense effort to enunciate and emerged in faintly strangled tones.

"You beg leniency and attempt to bargain by offering nothing in return? Whereas marriage," Xavier clarified succinctly, "will be adequate recompense for me dropping all charges against your father." He added in dry, mocking tones, "And clearing his gambling debts."

For a moment she lost the power to think as erotic images filled her mind, images she'd never been able to erase…. Words tumbled from her lips. "I don't want to marry you."

"Then we have nothing to talk about."

Welcome to the April 2010 collection of fabulous Presents stories for your indulgence!

About to lose his kingdom, Xavian will bed his new queen, but could she be his undoing? Find out in the first installment of our sizzling DARK-HEARTED DESERT MEN miniseries, *Wedlocked: Banished Sheikh, Untouched Queen* by Carol Marinelli. They're devastating, dark-hearted and looking for brides!

Why not enjoy two fabulous stories in one with *Her Mediterranean Playboy* by exciting authors Melanie Milburne and Kate Hewitt. Be seduced under the Mediterranean sun, where wild playboys tame their mistresses!

Isobel has never forgotten the night Brazilian millionaire Alejandro Cabral took her innocence, but when he discovers she had his daughter, he'll stop at nothing to claim her again in *The Brazilian Millionaire's Love-Child* by author Anne Mather.

Why not unwind with a sexy story of seduction and glamour—Xavier DeVasquez will have innocent Romy slipping between his sheets one more time in Helen Bianchin's *Bride, Bought and Paid For.* Sally must become Zac's mistress on demand or risk ruin in Jacqueline Baird's *Untamed Italian, Blackmailed Innocent!* And billionaire Lorenzo Valente vows to have his wedding night in *The Blackmail Baby* by Natalie Rivers.

Look out for the next tantalizing installment of DARK-HEARTED DESERT MEN in May with Jennie Lucas's *Tamed: The Barbarian King!*

The glamour, the excitement, the intensity just keep getting better!

Helen Bianchin
BRIDE, BOUGHT
AND PAID FOR

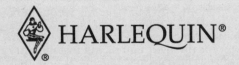

TORONTO • NEW YORK • LONDON
AMSTERDAM • PARIS • SYDNEY • HAMBURG
STOCKHOLM • ATHENS • TOKYO • MILAN • MADRID
PRAGUE • WARSAW • BUDAPEST • AUCKLAND

Recycling programs
for this product may
not exist in your area.

ISBN-13: 978-0-373-12907-2

BRIDE, BOUGHT AND PAID FOR

First North American Publication 2010.

Copyright © 2009 by Helen Bianchin.

www.eHarlequin.com

Printed in U.S.A.

All about the author...
Helen Bianchin

HELEN BIANCHIN grew up in New Zealand, an only child possessed by a vivid imagination and a love for reading. After four years of legal-secretarial work, Helen embarked on a working holiday in Australia where she met her Italian-born husband, a tobacco share farmer in far north Queensland. His command of English was pitiful, and her command of Italian was nil. Fun? Oh yes! So, too, was being flung into cooking for workers immediately after marriage, stringing tobacco and living in primitive conditions.

It was a few years later when Helen, her husband and their daughter returned to New Zealand, settled in Auckland and added two sons to their family. Encouraged by friends to recount anecdotes of her years as a tobacco share farmer's wife living in an Italian community, Helen began setting words on paper, and her first novel was published in 1975.

Creating interesting characters and telling their stories remains as passionate a challenge for Helen as it did in the beginning of her writing career.

Spending time with family, reading, and watching movies are high on Helen's list of pleasures. An animal lover, Helen says her Maltese terrier and two Birman cats feel her study is as much theirs as hers.

CHAPTER ONE

A BLUSTERY rain-shower whipped around the tram as it rode steel tracks towards the heart of Melbourne city.

The month of October in the southern hemisphere rested on the cusp between spring and summer, neither one nor the other, and tended to provide brilliant sunshine followed by rain with matching temperatures in contrary variation on the same day.

Rain and cool temperatures seemed incredibly appropriate, Romy decided with unaccustomed cynicism as the tram slid to a halt and disgorged several passengers before crossing the bridge spanning the Yarra River.

Tall inner-city buildings of varied design rose as concrete and glass sentinels, and she alighted at the next tram stop, caught a break in traffic and reached the pavement.

The nerves in her stomach clenched into a painful ball as she crossed the next intersection and entered the marble-tiled foyer of an imposing office building. Given a choice, she'd have preferred to deal with a class filled with hormone-charged, testosterone-fuelled recalcitrant teenage students who'd decided to give their English teacher the hardest day on record than confront the man who held her father's fate in his hands.

Of Spanish origin, New York born and bad boy made good, Xavier DeVasquez was an electronics whizz whose skills had elevated him to one of the world's wealthiest top five hundred. A man reputed for his cut-throat business methods. A force to be reckoned with in the boardroom… and the bedroom.

As she should know, she acknowledged silently, and endeavoured to quell the icy shiver feathering the length of her spine as the past three years vanished in the blink of an eye, providing startlingly vivid recall of a social charity event attended by several top employees of the DeVasquez Corporation, of which her father had been one. Head of the accountancy department, Andre Picard had been accompanied that evening by his wife and daughter, but it had been Romy who had drawn Xavier DeVasquez's attention.

The news media had failed to depict the degree of electric sexual chemistry the man exuded in person. On reflection, she hadn't stood a chance. Too many years spent studying to be a schoolteacher had meant a meagre social existence confined mainly to the company of girlfriends in the little free time she had permitted herself.

To suddenly have had someone of Xavier DeVasquez's calibre express a personal interest in her had been exciting. To discover he'd wanted to see her again, almost beyond belief. He'd had his pick of women, yet he'd chosen to spend time with *her*. When she'd asked why, he'd merely smiled and said he admired her lack of artifice.

Twelve weeks and three days. Romy could still remember the number of hours, the minutes.

She'd fallen in love with him. So soon, *too* soon, ignoring the faint niggle of disquiet that it wasn't real, *couldn't* be real. A fantasy of shared laughter, dinners, the theatre, a movie she'd wanted to see. Their parting kiss at evening's end, and the knowledge mere kisses would never be enough. The night she had gone back to his apartment and willingly into his bed...an innocent who had gifted him her virginity, her heart, her soul. And moved in with him the next day.

The affair had lasted three months before she'd made what became the ultimate mistake. At dawn's first opalescent glow, after a long night of lovemaking, she had told him that she loved him. Only to shatter into a thousand tiny pieces when he'd merely brushed his lips to her temple and said he didn't do *love*.

It had taken tremendous effort to calmly leave, to refuse his calls, accept a teaching position in another country and attempt to forget his existence.

Impossible, when his image had taunted her in vivid dream form through the long, lonely nights, and his name, together with photographic evidence appeared in the media relating yet another business coup, or a picture of him with a stunning female at his side had been displayed on a social page.

It had been her mother's fight against a progressive form of cancer two years later which had brought Romy home on three month's compassionate leave. An incredibly sad time, after which Andre had insisted she return to fulfil the remaining year of her teaching contract.

At first she'd been reluctant to leave him, but his reassurance had been convincing, which, together with the promised support of a few close family friends, helped ease her mind.

Her father's desperate bid to ensure his wife's every comfort had involved expensive treatments, the highest quality of care, and the fact he'd succeeded was laudable. Maxine Picard had gone to her grave unaware of the price her husband had paid, or the sequence of events which was to follow.

Who could have predicted the stock market crash that sent Andre Picard to the wall? Worse, that a once honourable man would stoop to defraud, then compound the crime with a desperate gambling bid in an effort to regain financial security.

Even Romy could have told her father it was a recipe for disaster, had she known.

Except it had only been when her teaching contract had ended and she'd returned to Melbourne to take up a new teaching position on home ground that she'd learnt the true state of her father's affairs.

Everything sold, including the small apartment which had replaced the family home following Maxine's death, the car, furniture and possessions.

Chilling to learn Andre had been arrested, charged and was awaiting trial with a prison sentence a certainty. None of which he'd revealed in letters, emails or intermittent telephone contact during her absence.

Instead, he'd deliberately waited until a week after her return before confiding the grim facts. A week in which she'd leased a furnished apartment, purchased a car, and taken up her new teaching position.

How could you have been so careless? were words she'd barely refrained from uttering…followed closely by *what were you thinking?*

Except the tired, care-worn man facing her looked *old* beyond his years, physically, mentally and emotionally beaten.

Instead, she'd swung into action, verifying fact, attempting to negotiate, but to no avail. Not surprising, given her father's total debt ran into millions…*plural*. A horrifying situation with no foreseeable way out. Except *one*…a personal appeal to Xavier DeVasquez as a last-ditch effort.

Phone calls, messages left, each more urgent than the last. Messages Xavier DeVasquez's PA assured were relayed. Except none elicited a return.

Which left Romy two options...and giving up wasn't one of them.

Three years teaching English to children in under-privileged areas had fashioned her into the young woman she'd become. At twenty-seven, she was a long way from the trusting romantic who'd believed a man's charm to be genuine and spun a fantasy web that had no basis in reality.

A man she was determined to confront *today*...one way or another. Even if it meant resorting to unconventional methods.

Yet what other option did she have?

None whatsoever.

So...suck it up, she admonished silently as she checked the Directory Board and crossed to the bank of lifts.

All too soon an electronic cubicle arrived, and she stepped inside, depressed the appropriate floor button and took a steadying breath as she was transported to her destination.

Understated luxury was clearly evident as she stepped off the lift and crossed the plush carpet to Reception where a perfectly groomed young woman manned the modern desk.

Romy summoned a smile. 'Xavier is expecting me.'

'May I have your name?' Fingers were poised fractionally above the computer keyboard, ready to check an electronic appointment schedule.

Assertiveness was key, together with a degree of easy familiarity. 'This is a personal visit.'

'I need your name so I can alert Mr DeVasquez's PA.'

The words remained polite, but firm, and Romy merely slanted an eyebrow. 'And spoil the surprise?'

The receptionist's mouth thinned a little. 'The DeVasquez Corporation observes a strict procedure.'

This was going nowhere, and any access would be denied, sans brute force, unless she identified herself. 'Romy Picard.'

Fingers tapped in the relevant letters, and Romy caught the moment a return message appeared on the screen, for the receptionist's eyes widened and her features assumed a cool expression.

'Mr DeVasquez is unavailable.'

Polite words issued without warmth or the hint of a smile, Romy noted as she bit back a few impolite uncool words of her own she'd like to utter.

'In that case I'll take a seat.'

'I should clarify Mr DeVasquez is not available for the rest of the day.'

'Nevertheless I'll wait.'

At that moment the phone buzzed, and Romy crossed to a clutch of deep-cushioned chairs, selected one and sank gracefully into it.

There were magazines fanned across a glass-topped coffee table, and she took one and pretended an interest in the pages.

Face it, she remonstrated silently some twenty minutes later. *Waiting* was a fruitless exercise. Any attempt to face Xavier DeVasquez was going to take affirmative action.

Determination strengthened her resolve…that, and a slow anger simmering beneath the surface of her control.

Dammit, enough was *enough.*

She rose to her feet and walked past Reception towards a wide aperture, leading, she presumed, to a number of offices, one of which *had* to belong to Xavier.

'You can't go through there.'

The words were sharp and a little harried…concern

for the interruption, or fear of repercussion from Xavier DeVasquez himself?

Romy merely lifted her head and kept walking.

She made it halfway down the corridor into a luxury lounge area where an impeccably attired woman barred her progress.

'Please return to Reception.'

Xavier DeVasquez's PA?

Romy directed a levelled look that would have struck terror into the heart of any of her former students. 'Where I'll be forced to wait indefinitely?'

'Mr DeVasquez is in a meeting.'

'Really? Then he's due for a break.' She moved to bypass the woman, only to have her step in the same direction.

'I'll call security to have you removed,' came the firm response.

So she could, but it would take time…time Romy intended to use to her advantage.

There were two closed doors bracketing the lounge. Romy took a punt and chose the left, entering without knocking to discover an empty executive suite. She turned back, aware the PA had picked up the phone, and she caught the woman's distressed expression as she crossed the lounge. It took only seconds to reach the second door, and she felt a moment of elation as it opened beneath her touch.

Five men were seated at a curved rectangular conference desk, and Romy refused to be intimidated as five heads turned towards her, four pairs of eyes expressing varying degrees of surprise, interest and speculation.

With the notable exception of the man seated at the head of the desk, whose eyes captured and held her own.

Dark, dangerously so…*forbidding*.

Xavier sensed his associates' masked surprise at the

intrusion. No one, without exception, was permitted entry
into a boardroom meeting without Xavier DeVasquez's
approval.

At that moment his cellphone pealed, and he brushed
aside his PA's apology, then ended the call.

His gaze didn't move from her own, and Romy was supremely conscious of his strong facial bone structure, the
dark, almost black eyes, and fine lines fanning from their
outer edges. Thick black hair worn a fraction too long lent
him an air of leashed savagery…elemental and vaguely
primitive. A generous mouth…so incredibly sensual, she
could remember the ease with which it had captured her
own and robbed her of any *sane* thought she might have
had at the time.

Helpless. Utterly and completely helpless, she'd exulted
in his touch, *believing* his apparent rapture mirrored her
own…only to discover it to be a figment of her imagination.

Did he have any idea what it cost her to face him? Or
know that she'd give almost anything to avoid doing so?

'I don't believe you have an appointment.'

Romy's eyes glittered as she absorbed his drawled
rebuke, and her chin lifted fractionally.

'Difficult to achieve, when your PA refused my every
request to make one.'

'On my instruction.'

She inclined her head. 'Naturally.'

'We have nothing to discuss.'

'Yes, we do.' Her gaze speared his own. 'Here, *now*…or
in private.' She waited a beat. 'Your choice.'

There was a part of him that admired her tenacity, her
courage.

A security team was poised on the other side of the
door, awaiting his instruction to forcibly remove her

from the building. All he had to do was lift the phone and say the words.

Except he did neither.

Instead, he deliberately raked her petite frame, silently challenging her to drop her gaze, only to be met with unblinking icy resolve as startlingly blue eyes held steady beneath his encompassing scrutiny.

A fashionable grey dress worn over a black cotton polo top accentuated her slender frame. Thin black leggings adorned her legs, and soft leather boots with killer heels added inches to her naturally petite height.

The young woman standing before him was the antithesis of the rather naive innocent he remembered. Inherent strength emanated from her small frame, determination and a degree of defiance he reluctantly admired.

It led him to speculate what she might offer in a vain attempt to save her father's skin. A woman's known asset…the use of her body?

Something stirred deep within. A pleasing memory of innocent wonder and uninhibited delight, her generosity, the sweet fervour of her mouth. Genuine, not a calculated act.

Heaven knew he'd become bored with his recent female companions and their predictable *modus operandi*. Practiced sycophants who used every known guise to attract his attention in a game as old as time.

Romy Picard could prove an interesting diversion. He'd blocked off every avenue of contact available to her… except one. And made it extremely difficult, almost impossible for her to circumvent. Yet she hadn't disappointed, and there was a part of him that applauded her persistence.

Xavier made a split-second decision, lifted the interoffice phone, and issued his PA with instructions to accommodate Romy Picard until the meeting's conclusion.

During which his eyes never left her own, and she refused to look away. Instead, she merely inclined her head, then turned and exited the room.

The cool, composed persona was a sham, one she maintained as she crossed to a comfortable leather chair and sank gracefully into its cushioned depths. Romy selected a magazine at random, studied the index, then chose an article and pretended interest in a stock-market graph.

She should have experienced a mild sense of elation at having succeeded in gaining an audience with Xavier DeVasquez. Except there was only anxiety existent, and a feeling of dread.

Ridiculous, she rationalized, when she'd dealt with rebellious young teens in a classroom of misfits and miscreants whose command of the English language comprised sassy belligerence in a deliberate attempt to diminish her authority. She'd achieved the unexpected, in a hard-won fight for the kind of mutual respect that promoted a degree of enthusiasm for learning. Because she cared enough to take the knocks in order to gain the end result.

Whether she could expect to win any form of reprieve for her father was something else…but she had to *try*.

Romy replaced the magazine and selected another, pretending interest in current electronic technology, when there was nothing further from her mind.

How long before Xavier concluded the meeting?

A hollow laugh rose and died in her throat. Five minutes—an hour…what difference did it make?

Thirty minutes and counting, she perceived when four men exited the conference room and acknowledged the CEO's PA before entering the corridor leading out to Reception.

A phone beeped on the PA's desk, and Romy quelled the sudden twist of nervous tension gripping her stomach as the PA uttered a few quiet words and stood to her feet.

'Mr DeVasquez will see you now.'

CHAPTER TWO

OKAY, she could do this. After all, what was the worst that could happen?

So why did each consecutive step towards the conference room feel as if she was walking to her doom?

Get over it, she cautioned silently as the PA lightly rapped the door, then immediately opened it and announced Romy's presence. Romy entered and heard the faint snick as the door closed behind her, and she unconsciously lifted her chin as she prepared to do battle with the man who'd condescended to allow her a few minutes of his time.

Xavier DeVasquez stood at the far end of the conference room. His height and breadth of shoulder accentuated by fine tailoring as he appeared engrossed in the scene beyond the floor-to-ceiling plate glass.

In profile, his facial features bore a chiselled look, the strong line of his jaw, sculptured cheekbones, and she felt a constriction in her throat as he turned towards her.

Arresting, he emanated a compelling power that was almost primitive, and she held his gaze as eyes dark as sin speared her own.

'You have five minutes.' The soft drawl held a hint of

purpose Romy chose to ignore as she retrieved an envelope from her bag and extended it towards him.

'You'll find a certified cheque attached to a detailed payment schedule for the balance my father owes.' The cheque wiped out her life savings and tabled payments that would extend *way* into the future.

His expression remained unchanged as he extracted the slim document and skimmed the amount of the cheque before perusing the legally assembled phrases. Each passing second seemed timeless as he read the words with unhurried ease, and the nerves in her stomach tightened into a painful ball when he tossed the document onto his desk.

'The repayment schedule you present includes a proportion of your father's estimated future earnings.' His voice held a dangerous softness that lifted the hairs on the back of her neck. 'No one will employ him in his former capacity given he's been charged with fraud.'

'They would, if you accept the repayment terms and drop all charges against him.'

'Your loyalty is admirable, but severely misplaced.'

The words held an accent-inflected drawl that did little to diminish their harshness, and her chin lifted fractionally.

'There were extenuating circumstances.'

He inclined his head in acknowledgement. 'Submitted in detail by your father's legal team.'

She regarded him steadily. 'Have you no compassion? Does fifteen years of loyal service count for nothing?'

'Had your father approached me and confided his difficulty in coping with crippling medical expenses, I could have made certain allowances. Instead, he chose to defraud, then compound it by racking up extensive gambling debts.' His expression hardened and his eyes seared her own. 'The DeVasquez Corporation offers strict but fair contracted

terms of employment. The consequences of flouting those
terms are clearly defined.'

For a wild, unbidden moment she had a desperate need
to pick up the nearest object and *hurl* it at him. Perhaps he
sensed her intention, for one dark eyebrow slanted and his
eyes became watchful. Such an action would be pure folly,
and instead she drew in a deep breath in a need for calm.

'Your rise and rise in the financial ranks is well tabled.
Your methodology known to be mercilessly ruthless.' She
waited a beat, then offered a deliberately sweet smile.
'Would your professional ethics bear intense scrutiny?'

A deadly silence encroached the room…electric, heart-
stopping. Except she refused to shift her gaze.

'You choose to insult me?' The words were deceptively
mild, but only a fool would dismiss their lethal intent.
There were corners cut, authority skirted, and a few early
dealings that had just skimmed beneath the legal line, but
he'd made generous recompense and his conscience was
clear…on all counts.

Romy experienced the strangest feeling: the floor tilted
slightly beneath her feet. Crazy, when she was on a high floor
of a concrete-and-steel building in downtown Melbourne!

Reaction, she assured herself silently. *Tension,* and a few
other emotions she determined not to explore as she marshalled strength of will.

Xavier took a cellphone from his pocket, keyed in a few
numbers, yet delayed activating the call as he regarded her
with chilling intensity. 'Do you really want to be escorted
onto the street?'

It was all Romy could do to control the sudden thumping
of her heart, unaware its heavy beat was clearly visible in
the pulse at the base of her throat as she held his gaze and
offered quietly, 'Threatening me isn't going to work.'

Silence hung suspended in the confines of the conference room, and she was conscious of every breath she
took as she waited for his reaction…certain he would
call her bluff.

For an age he merely subjected her to an all-encom-
passing appraisal, almost daring her to lower her gaze
and back down.

'No?'

He was a powerful force, one only a fool would disre-
gard…yet she refused to subjugate herself. If this was a
battle of wills, then she'd fight him to the bitter end.

'Three years ago you chose to cut and run,' Xavier
reminded her with deceptive mildness. 'And refused to ac-
knowledge any of my calls.'

Her eyes deepened to a brilliant sapphire. 'I'm surprised
you remember.'

Yet he did, more vividly than he was prepared to admit. Her
sweet mouth, the taste of her, the way she fit in his arms…
her smile, how her eyes lit up with pleasure whenever she
was in his presence.

He'd been her first lover, Xavier reflected. A fact that
had alternately delighted and dismayed him, for he'd
always dealt with women who knew the score and that
what he offered them was a pleasant interlude for however
long the relationship lasted, with no strings attached.

Romy had been different. Something he'd only begun
to realise after she had ended their brief affair. That had
been a rare, almost unknown occurrence, for in the past it
had been *he* who had called time, presented a parting gift
and moved on.

'What of your father's gambling debts?' Xavier pursued.
'Do you intend presenting his loan shark with a similar

deal?' He was already aware of the facts, except he wanted to hear them directly from her.

Romy bore his appraisal with equanimity, holding those dark almost black eyes in a determined effort not to be diminished in any way. 'Yes.'

'You have to know they won't buy it.' Quiet, deliberately stark words that accelerated her anxiety factor to new heights.

She'd already paid over a reasonable sum, but it had been made painfully clear what would happen if the outstanding balance wasn't paid on time.

'They might if I can negotiate reasonable terms with you.'

His eyes narrowed. 'You don't have the means to negotiate.' Didn't she know what she was up against? Or fully realize the consequences her father faced at the hands of a loan shark, who, after subjecting Andre Picard to a brutal lesson, would have no scruples in enforcing the lesson on Andre's daughter?

'That's your final answer?' Each word uttered caused her immeasurable pain, evidenced in the paleness of her features, the pulse jumping at the base of her throat.

Xavier bit back a pithy oath…more in anger at the situation she found herself in, than sympathy for the man who'd inadvertently put her there.

'Your expectation of my generosity is too high.'

'How much *too high*?'

She had courage, a quality he admired. Except she was way off base if she imagined any help he might be predisposed to offer came without a price.

Every risk Xavier took, and he admitted to many along the way, involved deliberate calculation. It was the basis of his success, the code by which he ran his business interests.

He knew all the angles, every devious aspect of human nature. Hadn't he worked them to his advantage in his early days on the streets of New York? It was also the reason no woman had managed to capture his heart as he climbed high among the social echelon.

Yet recently he'd experienced an unaccustomed restlessness. He owned a luxury mansion in one of Melbourne's prime waterfront suburbs, houses and apartments in various cities around the world, his own jet, expensive cars, an art collection worth millions. All he had to do was indicate he needed a woman in his bed, and several lined up to please him, aware the gift of jewellery and an all-expenses-paid sojourn in a spa resort were the only price he was prepared to pay.

While his business interests continued to challenge him, his personal life had become predictable, even boring. Was he sliding towards a mid-life crisis in his late thirties? Evaluating what he *really* wanted when, if appearances meant anything, he had it all?

In spite of the acquired sophistication, his generosity to select charitable causes, and the numerous acquaintances who sought his attention, his favour, he retained a degree of cynicism. Aware there were few women who would see past the size of his bank balance.

He owned a multi-national business enterprise, yet there was no child of his blood to take the reins in future and forge a dynasty.

His eyes narrowed thoughtfully as he regarded the young woman facing him. Affection, sexual compatibility...weren't those qualities realistically attainable in a relationship? And honesty...a quality Romy Picard possessed in spades.

'What if I were to put forward a proposal?'

For a moment she was prepared to swear her heart stopped beating. 'Proposing *what,* precisely?' The query held caution and an elevated degree of suspicion.

'Involving you.'

No. The word echoed through her mind as a silent scream. He was toying with her, like a butterfly in captivity as he waited for the moment he would pin her to the wall.

'I don't enter the equation.'

He continued to study her in silence, until she felt close to hitting him. Had he any idea how impossibly *angry* she was at having to confront him? In normal circumstances, she'd take extreme pleasure in telling him to go to *hell.*

'No?' Xavier posed with deceptive mildness. 'You represent the only tangible entity your father possesses of any worth to me.'

Something deep inside curled into a tight, painful ball, and she wanted nothing more than to turn and walk from the room, the building…anything to escape the compelling man who held her father's fate in his hands.

'You're suggesting I become a form of payment in human kind?' Each word took immense effort to enunciate and emerged in faintly strangled tones.

'Your words, not mine.'

His drawled voice held an indolence that caused the pulse at the base of her throat to quicken to a hammered beat.

'Prostitute myself by becoming your current mistress?'

'And bear me a child,' Xavier continued silkily.

It took enormous effort to resist the urge to slap his face, and for a heart-stopping moment time stood still, becoming a suspended entity when electric awareness pulsed heavily in the air.

Restrained anger emanated from her slender frame, and her eyes darkened to a vivid blue sapphire. 'Are you *insane?*'

'You beg leniency and attempt to bargain by offering nothing in return?'

Her eyes speared his, their blue depths intensely fiery

with incredible fury. 'What you're suggesting amounts to blackmail.'

'I prefer to call it a negotiated deal between two consenting adults.'

'Bastard.'

His eyebrows rose. 'Erroneous,' he relayed in a musing drawl. 'Given my parents were married at the time of my birth.' The fact his father had abandoned mother and child within weeks no longer seemed relevant, or that his mother had been forced to do menial work for long hours in order to survive a trailer-park existence, and had died young.

Romy took a deep, calming breath, aware it didn't come close to enough. Did he have any idea how much she wanted to rail against him? Even in her most trying moments in the classroom with students from hell, she hadn't come this close to physically lashing out. And that was saying something!

'You demand too much.'

He rose and indicated the door. 'Then we have nothing more to discuss.'

Words temporarily failed her, and she could only look at him with stark disbelief. 'You're asking me to become pregnant with your child,' she demanded with incredulity. 'Give it up after birth...then be cast out of its life?'

'Why would I cast a wife aside?'

The colour leeched from her face. 'What do you mean— *wife?*'

'Marriage,' Xavier clarified succinctly. 'Adequate recompense for me dropping all charges against your father,' he added in dry mocking tones. 'And clearing his gambling debts.'

For a moment she lost the power to *think* as erotic images filled her mind...images she'd never been able to erase, and words tumbled from her lips without thought. 'I don't want to marry you.'

'Consider the advantages.'

'At the moment, I can't think of *one.*'

Was that a quick gleam of amusement she glimpsed on his face or merely a trick of the light?

'No?'

Romy swept his impressive form a deliberate appraisal, and successfully tamped down the unbidden emotion threatening to consume her body. 'What we shared wasn't anything special.'

Liar, she silently castigated. *Once,* just once she'd attempted to erase his lovemaking from her mind by superimposing it by having sex with someone else…and the memory still gave her cause to regret the experience.

Xavier tamped down the urge to pull her in close and take possession of her mouth, to tame her fine anger and turn it into purring pleasure. Instead, he reached out a hand and trailed light fingers down her cheek, then he cupped her chin and eased his thumb-pad gently over the soft fullness of her lower lip. He watched her eyes darken and sensed the faint hitch in her breath.

So much for thinking she was immune to his touch! Strength of spirit ensured she stood perfectly still, her eyes steady as she held his gaze, and she wondered if he had any inkling just how much it cost her to do so.

'You want a deal for your father,' Xavier reiterated quietly. 'I've offered a solution. Take it or leave it.'

The thought of her father having to appear in court again, be escorted under police guard to prison, suffer indignities, fear, not to mention several years incarceration, possibly *die* there, was more than Romy could bear.

'Do you need me to spell out what form of reminder the

loan shark will serve Andre, and ultimately *you,* if payment isn't forthcoming on time?' Xavier queried and saw her features pale.

She had until midnight tomorrow to produce a large sum of money neither she nor Andre could scrape together.

Face it, she reminded herself grimly. Every possible resource had been explored. Xavier DeVasquez was their last hope for any form of rescue package that would help her father.

A hollow sensation settled in her stomach as desperate reality hit home. She had a choice, which was really no choice at all. The question had to be—did she have sufficient courage to take what Xavier offered? Yet how could she *not?*

The faint burr of his phone intruded, and he picked it up, listened, offered a curt instruction, then he ended the call.

There was little to be gained from his expression, and she didn't even attempt to hazard a guess as she bore his measured scrutiny.

'I have an important meeting scheduled.' He paused fractionally. 'Your answer, Romy?'

This was it, she recognized with a sense of fatalism. She'd come this far and would gain much—at considerable personal cost—if she agreed to the deal. A deal which didn't need to be a life sentence, for marriage carried an escape clause. There was always the option of divorce.

Her eyes sparked brilliant blue fire. 'Yes…damn you.'

For a brief second she thought she glimpsed humour in those dark eyes, then it was gone.

'I don't recall you being quite so verbally explicit,' Xavier drawled and watched as she made a concentrated attempt to rein in her anger.

'It's the effect you have on me.' Calm, she had to remain

calm. Difficult when she was filled with mixed emotions…
not one of them *good.*

'I need a contact phone number before you walk out the
door.' His voice was like silk and sent her stress levels up
a few notches.

'I'll leave it with your PA.'

Xavier withdrew a card and handed it to her. 'I prefer
to keep my personal life and business matters separate.'

Romy took the pen he offered, scrawled her mobile
number onto the back of the card, and placed both on his
desk, then she turned, walked unseeing out to main
Reception and took a lift down to the ground level.

She'd succeeded in gaining her father a reprieve.

It should have felt like victory…instead it felt like hell.

CHAPTER THREE

THE phone pealed as Romy was about to step into the shower back at her St Kilda apartment, and she quickly pulled on a robe then raced into the bedroom to pick up her mobile, checked caller ID and failed to recognize the number.

'Romy.'

Xavier.

There was no doubting the male voice, or to whom it belonged, and she drew in a deep breath, then slowly released it.

'What do you want?'

'We're due to meet with my lawyer in half an hour.'

He moved fast…but what else did she expect?

'I have plans,' she said coolly. She didn't, except he wasn't to know that.

'Do you really want to do this the hard way?'

If only she didn't have to do it at all!

'I'll be at your apartment in fifteen minutes.'

'You don't know the address.' Empty words, given he'd already cut the connection.

A soft oath escaped her lips in the knowledge he had the means to discover almost anything he wanted to know including her new place of residence.

For a few timeless seconds she considered slipping out before Xavier arrived only to give up the idea almost as soon as it occurred.

Fool, she silently berated herself as she stepped into the shower stall. Such an action could lead to financial suicide.

The in-house phone pealed as Romy was putting the finishing touches to her hair, and she picked up, identified Xavier and quickly announced she was on her way down.

Tailored trousers, neatly buttoned blouse beneath a jacket, killer heels, with her hair swept into a careless knot held in place by a large clasp. Casual, yet chic. Minimal make-up.

Good to go, she decided as she picked up her keys and tossed them into her clutch as she exited her apartment.

Xavier was waiting for her when the lift doors slid open at ground level, and she tamped down the sudden quiver in her stomach at the sight of him.

He bore the look of a man whose sophisticated exterior belied the dangerous earthy quality that lay beneath the surface.

Black trousers, an open-necked shirt and a black soft-leather jacket replaced the formal business suit. Attire which did little to lessen the lethal impact of the man.

For a wild moment she considered telling him she'd changed her mind. Except doing so wasn't an option.

Her chin lifted fractionally, and she met and held his level gaze with equanimity as she crossed to his side.

Stilettos added inches to her petite height, but even so the top of her head barely reached his shoulder. Three years ago she'd felt protected, whereas now it merely enhanced her vulnerability.

Did he pick up on it? Possibly. *Vulnerable* wasn't an emotion she wanted to impart.

'I hope this won't take long,' Romy began, and saw his eyes narrow.

'We settle the legal issues,' Xavier reiterated as he ushered her through the foyer to the security-controlled entry. 'Then we share dinner.'

They exited the building, and he indicated a sleek Mercedes Maybach resting in a nearby reserved-parking bay.

'I don't want to have dinner with you.' Romy waited as he disengaged the locking mechanism and opened the front passenger door.

'Tough,' he dismissed coolly as she moved past him and slid into the seat.

The door closed with a refined clunk, and she delayed her response until he slipped into the adjoining seat.

'I get the need for a pre-nup,' she managed with deliberate calm as her eyes speared his. 'As to the marriage…when do you envisage the ceremony will take place?'

Xavier engaged the engine and spared her a cool glance. 'This weekend.'

Her stomach did a slow somersault as he eased the car out onto the street and headed towards the city.

'Why so soon?' Her life was moving so fast it felt as if she'd boarded a runaway train!

'You need me to spell it out?'

It was simple maths: Andre needed a large sum of money *fast;* Romy represented the surety…and Xavier didn't negotiate an unsecured deal.

Dear God, the enormity of what she'd agreed to do acquired momentous proportion!

'You've informed Andre?'

Romy closed her eyes, then opened them again. 'Yes.' Only that she'd succeeded in clearing his debts…not the price she had to pay. Although no matter what spin she put on it, her father was unlikely to be fooled. Nor would he approve her decision. The reason she had elected to relay the details to him in person.

Two weeks ago she'd been looking forward to returning home, reconnecting with her father, and had viewed the challenge of a different school, new students with enthusiasm.

Her life, as she'd envisaged it to be, had quickly taken a dramatic about-turn...irrevocably, she reflected pensively. At least, for a while.

Marriage. What young woman didn't dream of meeting *the* man of her dreams, falling in love, and living the *happy ever after?*

Once, more than three years ago, she'd imagined she was living the dream, only to discover the man she loved wasn't on the same page...let alone reading the same book!

Now, through circumstance, she was soon to be legally linked to him in a loveless union based on thinly disguised blackmail.

What on earth was she getting herself into?

A faintly hysterical laugh rose and died in her throat. Emotional insanity...nothing more, or less.

The question had to be...could she survive with dignity and some of her emotions intact?

A few years tops, she reminded herself. Then she'd file for divorce. Irreconcilable differences, a sufficiently ambiguous blanket covering a multitude of sins.

The image of a baby filled her mind, and her heart plummeted along with her resolve. A child...how could she give up a child? Share custody, time, not be *there* every day, every night, only when designated by a court of law?

But what if there wasn't a child? What if she took steps to ensure she didn't conceive?

Would Xavier choose divorce in order to select any one of several women who would bear him a child?

'Your silence is telling.'

The faintly accented drawl interrupted her introspection, and she turned her head to offer him a cool look.

'Really?'

Xavier checked the rear-vision mirror, indicated and drew the car into the kerb, killed the engine, then he turned towards her.

'If you're having second thoughts, now's the time to say so.'

Deadly calm words which ricocheted inside her brain and succeeded in freezing the blood in her veins.

Oh dear Lord. What was she *doing?*

She couldn't afford to lose control…or change the goal posts in this diabolical game.

Any self-indulgent time-out was merely a whiplash reaction. So…*get over it.*

'Your call, Romy.'

When thrust between a rock and a hard place…what did you choose?

There was only one answer she could give. 'I imagine your lawyer is waiting for us,' she managed quietly.

'That's it?'

She gathered the tenuous threads of her emotions together and gave an affirmative. 'Yes.'

Money, in excess, opened doors and provided services not usually offered outside normal business hours, Romy perceived a short while later as she preceded Xavier into a sumptuous office suite, where, introductions complete, she sank into a cushioned leather chair, listened carefully to the lawyer's explanation of relevant documents, aware every possible contingency was covered in watertight legalese.

She almost baulked when the moment came to attach her signature. The enormity of her commitment seemed overwhelming, and for a wild moment she considered standing to her feet and walking out.

Except the ramification of such an action would be prohibitive and would destroy everything she'd strived to achieve.

So…pick up the offered pen and *sign,* a tiny voice prompted, and without further thought she did just that. Then she carefully replaced the pen on the desk.

The following minutes became a blur as both men conversed with an easy familiarity that spoke of friendship, and she rose to her feet automatically when Xavier indicated the session was at an end. She even smiled and offered a few polite words as the lawyer escorted them to the lift.

There wasn't a word she could say as the lift took them down to ground level, and she bore Xavier's unwavering scrutiny with equanimity.

'I'll take a cab back to my apartment.'

'No,' he refuted quietly. 'We'll eat, then visit your father.'

'I'm not hungry.'

'Opposing me just for the hell of it?' Xavier's voice held a touch of cynical humour, and she sent him a cursory look that spoke volumes.

He chose a restaurant at Southbank where the food was excellent and surpassed only by the dedicated service.

'Shall I order for you?'

Romy offered him a speaking glance and pretended intense interest in the menu. Food of any kind held little appeal, although there was a need to select something, and she chose bruschetta, declined wine and settled for a non-alcoholic spritzer.

Lunch had comprised a slice of toast with honey, followed by a banana…all she'd felt her stomach could digest at the time.

There was, she perceived, nothing wrong with his appetite as he ordered a starter and followed it with a main. A dish she'd favoured during the brief time they'd been together.

Coincidence? Or was it a deliberate choice?

Like she cared!

Yet something tightened inside her stomach that he might have remembered a time when they'd shared food, forking a tempting morsel for sampling, delighting in knowing they'd share so much more at evening's end.

Then she had been relaxed and in tune with him, just living to please and be pleasured.

A delicious tremor slid the length of her spine at the unbidden image, painfully vivid as memory resurfaced.

'You've begun a new contract at a high school in the northern suburbs.'

Romy spared him a questioning look. 'Your PA was instructed to determine the precise location and relevant details?'

Xavier lifted an eyebrow. 'It bothers you that I did so?'

Yes. Although she'd expected it of him. Xavier had long gained a reputation for sourcing every detail, even the most seemingly inconsequential. Very little, if anything, escaped him, and heads were known to roll should any of his subordinates fail to deliver. *Life* and his climb to the top had fashioned him into the man he'd become.

'Then you'll be aware I have a contract to fullfil.'

'A contract isn't set in stone,' he reminded her, and caught the way her eyes blazed blue fire.

'I teach, it's what I do,' Romy vouchsafed.

He leaned back in his chair and regarded her steadily. 'There's no need for you to continue working.'

'What else would you have me do? Become a social butterfly who spends her days having beauty treatments and shopping?' She sent him a quelling look. 'Forget it.'

'You prefer attempting to impart enthusiasm for knowledge into young minds, controlling their behaviour, offering extra-curricular tutoring and immersing yourself in setting and marking numerous assignment papers?'

'Yes.' Among the students who slipped through the scholastic system, there were those who could excel, and she strived to give both at opposite ends of the scale her equal attention.

Statistics proved some would never make it, a fact which only made her try harder, to go beyond and above the call of duty.

'There are those who baulk at the theory of learning, yet excel in practice.'

'Such as yourself?'

'The cut and thrust in the real business world, the challenge to succeed against the odds provides an adrenalin rush coveted by many.'

'High risk, high maintenance.'

'You neglect to mention the rewards,' Xavier drawled, and she arched an eyebrow.

'The mansions, houses abroad, expensive cars?'

A faint smile teased the edges of his mouth. 'You forgot to include the women.'

She matched the faint mockery in his voice with droll cynicism. 'Of course…*women.*'

'There were not so many,' Xavier relayed with musing indulgence. 'And I ended each relationship before I began another.'

'For which you think you deserve brownie points?'

His smile verged on the indolent. 'You'd paint me as a careless rake?'

She managed a imperceptible shrug. 'If the cap fits.'

A waiter delivered coffee, and Xavier settled the bill.

They emerged onto the boardwalk to crisp cool air and an indigo sky sprinkled with a light dusting of stars.

Romy retrieved her cellphone and keyed in a series of digits, gave her location and ordered a taxi. Only to give a startled exclamation as the cellphone was taken from her hand and the call cancelled.

Anger rose to the fore as she shot Xavier a venomous glare. 'How dare you?' She reached for the phone. 'Give it back.'

'A taxi isn't an option.'

She closed her eyes, then opened them again. The temptation to lash out at him was almost impossible to resist. 'I'm going to visit my father...*alone,*' Romy asserted, sorely tried.

'No.'

Anger pumped from her in a fine red mist. 'What is it with you?'

He suppressed the urge to take possession of her sassy mouth and tame all that fiery rage into whimpering submission. And he would...soon.

'Do you really want to do this here?'

Realization of where they were, in a public place, people out enjoying the evening air and, oh, God, the interested looks they were garnering...had a sobering effect.

Her scorching glare had little effect, and she stepped to one side and strode—as well as one could stride in stiletto heels—towards the main road. Only to inwardly fume as he matched her pace with an easy grace.

The silence between them became a potent, volatile entity, one she refused to break as they reached the car.

For a brief moment Romy considered a final act of defiance, only to change her mind at the tempered warning evident in his dark eyes.

'Do you need the address?' Cool, stilted words, which had no effect whatsoever as Xavier released the car's locking mechanism.

'No.'

So he knew Andre's fall from grace had led to a small, barely adequate flat in a western suburb, a far cry from the lovely home her parents had occupied during Romy's youth.

She chose silence as Xavier traversed the inner city and took a route leading to one of numerous streets where red-brick houses were jammed close together on minuscule blocks of land.

The shabby home where Andre resided had long been converted into one-bedroom self-contained flats, a place her father would soon leave, if she had anything to do with it!

Her father's flat was reached from a narrow central hallway, and Andre's smile faltered as he opened the door, then disappeared as he saw the man standing at Romy's side.

'Xavier.' The greeting was cautious, polite, and Romy's stomach tightened into a painful knot as she gave her father an affectionate hug during the heavy silence which followed.

'Andre,' Xavier acknowledged, as her father stood to one side to allow them entry into an open-plan room comprising a lounge area and adjoining dining room.

Two single club chairs bracketed a small sofa, and Andre indicated them.

'Please, take a seat. Can I offer you some tea or coffee?'

Her heart tore a little at her father's attempt at normality in what had to be an unforeseen situation, one that would rapidly digress to extraordinary any time soon.

'I'll make it.'

In the kitchen she filled the electric kettle and set out cups and saucers, taking longer than necessary in order to delay rejoining both men.

She hadn't expected her father to easily accept her decision, and her fingers shook a little as she heard Andre's voice rise a little.

Time to go face the fallout, she decided as she placed everything on a tray and crossed the room, her head high, a smile firmly in place.

Andre viewed her in contemplative silence as she offered him coffee.

'You always consider your actions,' he declared, perplexed. 'Yet you're rushing headlong into a marriage in circumstances that are far too coincidental.' He was silent for several seconds as he searched Xavier's features. 'If I thought you had deliberately orchestrated this…' He faltered, momentarily unable to continue. 'It's unconscionable.'

Her heart ached for him, and she so badly wanted to fabricate something…*anything* that would help ease his mind. Except there was only pretence, and her father was too intelligent not to see through it.

'A permanent relationship should be sanctified by marriage,' Xavier revealed quietly. 'Or would you prefer I take Romy as my mistress?'

The silence in the room was a palpable entity, and as much as she wanted to rail against Xavier, to do so in her father's presence would only compound a bad situation.

In seeming slow motion she saw her father's features pale and take on an ashen tinge as his tortured eyes searched her own.

'I won't let you do this.'

There was only one way to go, and she took it as she clasped his hands between her own. 'I'm marrying Xavier this weekend,' she said gently. 'Will you honour me by being at my wedding?'

His eyes filled, and for a moment she thought he might break down, then he managed to regain a degree of composure. 'Can you give me your word you're doing this of your own free will?'

God forgive her, but what could she say other than—'Yes.'

It hurt to see him struggle to accept her decision, and for a moment she thought he meant to protest further, except after several long seconds he inclined his head.

'I won't disappoint you.' A sufficiently ambiguous claim that almost brought her undone.

Romy was unsure how she managed to get through the ensuing half hour before she indicated a need to leave. It was almost ten, and she had papers to mark. Besides which, it had been a hell of a day, and she desperately wanted the quiet solitude of her flat.

In the car she simply leant her head against the cushioned rest and momentarily closed her eyes as Xavier ignited the engine.

'Relax.'

'Sure, and that's going to happen any time soon.' She turned her head towards him and sent him a venomous glare. 'Do you have any idea how much I hated what went down in there just now?'

'It was better we approached Andre together.'

'Better for whom?'

He spared her a glance as he paused the car at an intersection. 'You.'

'I didn't need any support.'

'No?'

'Please,' she remonstrated, hating him afresh. 'Don't play the protector.'

'You don't see me in that role as your husband?'

His query was indolently deceptive, and there was nothing she could do to quell the sudden spear of pain.

'Like the title of *wife* is security against you taking a lover or three when you tire of me?'

'Why would I take a lover if my wife satisfies me?'

'That's a two-way street.'

'You doubt I can satisfy you?'

She remembered too well how he'd managed to satisfy her. Dammit, her body still reacted just *thinking* how it had *sung* in response to his touch.

He smiled as he eased the car into a main arterial road leading to St Kilda, and she focused her attention beyond the windscreen, aware of the passing traffic, the wide tree-lined thoroughfare.

It was a relief when he turned into Marine Parade and drew the car to a halt outside her apartment building.

Her hand was already on the seatbelt release, and the breath caught in her throat as she reached for the door clasp, only to have him frame her face with his hands.

He was close, much too close.

'What—'

'This.'

There wasn't time to complete the protest as his mouth closed over her own in a slow, sweeping kiss that tore at her resolve and shattered it.

For a wild moment she forgot everything except the feel and taste of him and the electric pulsing sensation throbbing through her body.

It was as if the past three years had ceased to exist, and

she was barely conscious of the faint groan that rose and died in her throat at her unbidden response.

She felt the stroke of his thumb along her jawline, sensed the increased pressure of his mouth, and she gave herself up to the sweet passion of his touch.

Magic, she accorded silently, unable to *think* as she became lost. Cast adrift from reality and flung heedlessly into a time and place where emotion ruled.

Until sanity returned, and she wrenched away from him, her eyes impossibly large as she attempted to control her ragged breathing. 'Don't—'

Xavier's eyes gleamed dark in the reflected street light.

Romy reached blindly for the door clasp, and he let her go, waiting until she had keyed her security code into the numeric pad and had passed through the foyer before he engaged the engine.

She was barely aware of the lift's swift passage until it slid to a halt at her floor, and she muttered a curse as she fumbled the key when she inserted it into the lock.

For heaven's sake…what was *wrong* with her?

Her mouth still tingled from his touch, and she put a hand to her still-racing heart as she closed the door behind her and leant against it.

What had just happened back there?

If she'd ever wondered about the sensuality they'd once shared…oh, call it what it was, she dismissed in silent chastisement…passion. Incandescent and primitive…emotion that took possession of the soul.

Hers, she admitted reluctantly. But not his.

For Xavier, she merely represented the bride price he was prepared to pay in order to gain a legitimate heir.

And to exact revenge against father and daughter, don't forget that, she reminded herself with cynicism.

It would be the height of folly to imagine otherwise. She pushed away from the door and drew in a deep, calming breath.

So take a reality check, why don't you?

She slipped out of her stilettos, shrugged off her jacket, crossed into the kitchen where she made a cup of strong coffee, then she set it down on the table, opened her leather satchel and turned her attention to marking student assignments.

It was after midnight when she crawled into bed and doused the light, convinced her brain was buzzing too much to enable an easy sleep.

Except she was wrong, and the next thing she remembered was waking to the early dawn light filtering through the shutters of her bedroom window.

CHAPTER FOUR

THE next day began with an alarm clock which didn't go off, ensuring Romy woke late, dressed hurriedly, gulped coffee on the run and took a banana to eat en route to the high school in the northern suburbs.

Traffic was heavy, and there were the usual delays at computer-controlled intersections.

Consequently, she arrived with bare minutes to spare before she was due in class. *Not* the ideal way to begin a day.

Worse, the few miscreants in class seemed bent on providing distraction, testing the new teacher on the block.

OK, so the English classics failed to inspire their attention, despite her every effort to provide modern, upbeat comparisons, and it became a morning where male testosterone vied with female hormones in a bid for witticism supremacy.

'So, Teach—like, who *is* this Will Shakespeare dude, anyway? And what does someone *dead* have anything to do with us?'

'Yeah. And what's with sonnets and couplets?'

'Like we *care?*'

Explaining the greats were an important part of literary history didn't seem to cut it.

'Bono, now, he's a dude with something to say.'

'Ice. Snoop Dogg,' a voice added.

'Seal.'

'Yeah,' endorsed a recalcitrant chorus, and Romy swung into idiomatic lingo with an ease that surprised them.

Be prepared, was an adhered-to motto when all else failed. She'd done her homework well, isolating verses from the literary greats and comparing them with gangsta rap idioms.

Not so different in translation, given the mores of different centuries, and she gave a silent *yes* in victory as the overt boredom underwent a change and emerging interest took its place.

Nothing was said. Overkill wasn't on the agenda.

At the end of class, she merely thanked them for attending and asked them to provide ten more comparisons for their next English class.

Lunch was eaten in the staffroom, whose occupants seemed grateful for the brief respite prior to taking on the afternoon.

Romy's cellphone beeped with an incoming text message as she ascended a flight of stairs en route to an afternoon class.

Xavier, she determined, alerting her he'd ring her at seven that evening. *Why?* she quickly keyed and received *wedding details* within a few seconds.

Romy bit back an unladylike oath, stowed the cellphone in her bag, summoned a smile and entered a classroom where several students either lolled against their desks or sat on them, and whose belligerent expressions promised a difficult session.

One teenager, he of the class clown species, made a conscientious point of addressing her as *Miz* too frequently with such faux-angelic regard she was sorely tempted to laugh, something she managed to avoid as she suggested he move to the front of the class and read two verses of Byron out loud.

An edict which saw him slide to the floor on his knees, bow his head in mock prayer and beseech—'Anything, *Miz,* but not Byron.'

'William Wordsworth,' Romy responded without hesitation. '"The Daffodils."' She waited a beat. 'In its entirety.'

A subtle irony that was lost as the class leafed to the index and turned to the section on Wordsworth.

Two lines in, the class clown lifted his head, looked heavenward, cursed, then uttered a pitiful, 'Sheesh, you have to be joking.'

'Begin again,' Romy instructed evenly. 'This time, restrain from adding your own comments.'

Did she win points? Doubtful. A smidgen of respect? Unlikely.

It came as a relief to wind up the school day, gather papers into her satchel and slip behind the wheel of her Mini Cooper.

There were things she needed to do, and persuading her father to exchange his meagre digs for her apartment held priority. Something which took a while, and involved his pride and her perspicacity until he reluctantly accepted her insistent decision to continue paying the monthly leasing fee. Relevant phone calls cemented the arrangement, making it a done deal before Andre could change his mind.

'Now?'

His incredulous query brought a determined smile as she reiterated, '*Now.* I'll help you pack.'

'Since when did you become so bossy?' His voice held a tinge of amusement, something she welcomed, and her answering grin was genuine.

'It's been a while.'

Not that there was much to fold into a suitcase, and she held back the tears as she saw just how little he'd kept from his former lifestyle. A framed wedding photograph, one of Romy the day she began school, another when she graduated. A treasured miniature crystal Waterford world globe, a gift to him from her mother, and clothes.

'I'll take the couch,' he said firmly as they entered her St Kilda apartment.

But only until her marriage to Xavier...the knowledge was uppermost, a fast-moving event planned to happen soon.

Much too soon, as Romy discovered when Xavier rang shortly after seven and relayed, after a brief greeting, 'I've arranged for a celebrant to conduct the marriage at six-thirty Friday evening. I suggest you pack and move here tomorrow.'

She counted to three...slowly. 'I'll transfer my belongings to the house on Thursday evening. I have classes on Friday.' One being the last for the afternoon. 'I won't be able to make it until six.'

'Romy.' His voice was like silk, and she ignored the silent warning evident.

'*Where,* precisely?'

She took a notepad, pen, and jotted down the address. Upmarket Brighton, in a street which overlooked the beach. Expensive real estate. Make that *very* expensive real estate. 'Thank you.' She cut the connection, summoned a smile and turned towards her father.

'Shall I put on a DVD? Refill your coffee?'

Andre indicated a chair close to his own. 'Come sit down for a while.'

It was easy to do his bidding, not so easy to relax.

'I won't pretend to believe the arrangement you've struck with Xavier is anything other than what it is,' her father offered tentatively. 'No matter that you once shared a brief relationship with him, never allow yourself to forget he's a ruthless man, and one you'd be advised not to cross.'

'You think I'm not aware of that?' Romy posed quietly.

Forty-eight hours from now she'd be Xavier's wife. She'd fulfil her end of the bargain…but on her terms. She didn't intend for him to hold *all* the cards in this diabolical game.

It was after ten when she retired to her room, and almost midnight before she finished fine-tuning the next day's assignments.

On the edge of sleep she conducted a mental review of her wardrobe, discarding the few good clothes she possessed as being unsuitable to wear to her wedding…which meant she needed to add shopping to her list of things to do.

Thursday proved to be one of *those* days. A day she weathered with true grit and determination.

There were few students who saw the need to learn the technicalities of English language usage. Yet their knowledge was tested, their grades counted, and at the end of the school year…it mattered.

Why? became an oft-asked query, usually accompanied by a groan of despair, when computer software held a dictionary, spell-check and grammar-check at the click of a mouse?

Besides, who cared?

With back-to-back classes, surviving the day became something of an endurance test, and Romy experienced a short-lived feeling of relief as she eased her Mini towards a suburban shopping centre where, after searching a number of boutiques, she discovered a lovely design in ivory voile, whose simplicity enhanced her slender curves. A scooped neckline, elbow-length sleeves, and a hemline that fell just below her knees.

Not exactly bride wear, it nevertheless was sufficiently stylish for a very small intimate wedding where the number of attendants were restricted to the bride and groom, the bride's father and Xavier's lawyer.

It was almost six when she entered her apartment to the welcome aroma of cooked food, and she crossed to her father's side, brushed her lips to his cheek, and offered an appreciative smile.

'Thanks. Smells great.'

'Spaghetti bolognaise with garlic bread,' Andre enlightened. 'Go wash up and we'll eat.'

She did, and she expounded on her day, asked about his, and insisted on dealing with the dishes before retreating to her bedroom in order to pack.

There seemed little point in transferring every item of clothing she possessed, and she simply placed what she'd need for a week into a capacious bag, then carried it into the lounge.

Her father cast her a look of concern, and his lips parted as if he would say something, only for them to close again.

Go, a silent voice prompted, and she did, offering a faint smile as she moved towards the front door. 'I won't be long.' An inane comment, if ever there was one... except *any* words she might utter right now seemed superfluous.

So she'd visit Xavier's Brighton home, say *hi,* deposit her bag...and leave. How difficult could it be?

There was no reason for the stirring of butterflies in her stomach as she hit the main road and made her way along the busy thoroughfare.

No reason at all, she assured herself. Xavier might not even be at home, and she could simply hand her bag to his housekeeper.

Sure, like that's going to happen, Romy thought as she closed the distance to his prestigious address.

By the time she drew the Mini to a halt before an imposing set of closed gates the nerves in her stomach had tightened into a painful ball.

What now? Where was the speakerphone to announce her presence?

At that moment the gates slid open, and she bit off a silent oath at the reality of electronic surveillance. A necessary precaution for the wealthy in today's era, she had to admit as she eased her car onto the illuminated semi-circular driveway.

A two-storied Tuscan-style mansion stretched across the block of land, and she caught a glimpse of landscaped gardens, shrubbery, in the time it took to reach the front entry. Wide double wood-panelled doors which opened as she closed off the engine.

Xavier's tall, broad frame was unmistakable as he crossed the tiled forecourt and reached for the car's door clasp as she released her seatbelt.

For a brief second, she resembled a frightened doe caught in the spotlight, he mused, watching as her expression assumed a bland mask.

'My bag is in the trunk.' Amazing, her voice sounded normal! She caught up her purse and slid out from behind the wheel as he retrieved her bag, then she preceded him into the spacious lobby.

She caught a glimpse of marble floor tiling, a wide, curved double staircase leading to an upper level, solid mahogany furniture, paintings adorning the walls.

Wealth, representing superb taste, was clearly evident, the crystal tiered chandelier linked to the high ceiling magnificent as it lit a lobby highlighted by wall sconces.

Xavier set her bag at the foot of the staircase, then indicated an open door to his right.

'I'll have Maria serve coffee.'

She wanted to say she couldn't stay, except he'd see it for the excuse it was. And she refused to give him the satisfaction.

'Thank you.' She could do this…exchange polite conversation over coffee, then she'd leave.

The large formal lounge was vaguely intimidating, and she wondered if his choice was deliberate.

Oh, for the love of heaven, get a grip, she bade herself silently.

He caught the slight edge of tension apparent and chose to ignore it as his housekeeper appeared with a tray.

Introductions complete, Maria poured steaming aromatic coffee into two cups before retreating from the room.

The need to say something…anything, seemed paramount in the ensuing silence.

'I've arranged for my father to take over my apartment,' Romy said quietly as she accepted a cup and saucer from his hand. 'Naturally, I'll maintain the lease.'

Xavier offered sugar and cream, both of which she refused. 'He's there now?'

She inclined her head and met his gaze with equanimity. 'Is this where I ask about your day?'

'Do you really want to know?'

'Give it a shot.'

The edges of his mouth lifted a little, and a glimmer of humour lit his dark eyes for a few seconds. 'Meetings, closing an important deal.' He waited a beat. 'Having my

PA organize accommodation at Peppers on the Mornington Peninsula for the weekend.'

Her heart missed a beat. They were going away? 'Is that necessary?'

'You thought we'd stay in?'

She didn't know what to think! 'It's hardly appropriate.'

One eyebrow rose. 'No?'

'It's not as if we're embarking on a real marriage.'

'Define *real*.' His voice was a silky drawl. 'I'm intrigued to hear your interpretation.'

Oh, hell, she'd fallen into that one! 'Do I need to spell it out?'

'Indulge me.'

'You want a verbal fencing match, go play with someone else,' Romy managed calmly.

'It seems I've chosen you.'

She was sassy, Xavier mused. Older, not only in years, and there were only a few, but there was a maturity existent that hadn't been apparent during their relationship.

The loss of her mother and her father's downfall had undoubtedly contributed, but it was more than that, and he wondered at the reason.

A love affair gone wrong?

Somehow that didn't sit too well, and he chose not to examine it in depth.

Romy sipped her coffee, then she carefully replaced her cup and saucer onto the tray. 'If you'll excuse me?' She rose to her feet. 'I have papers to mark.'

Not exactly a wise move, given he followed her action, and he stood too close, heightening her awareness of him to an alarming degree.

It wasn't fair. She had every reason to hate him…and she did. She really *did*. So what was with the spiralling sensation curling through her body? The increased pulse-beat, and the nerves clamoring inside her stomach like a silent cacophony?

Did he know?

Hell, she hoped not!

'You could stay.'

The drawled query almost brought her undone, and she lifted her chin and met those dark, enigmatic eyes.

'No.'

'Pity.'

He was amused, darn him, and she spared him an expressive glare that was more telling than mere words, then she turned and made her way to the front entrance, aware he walked at her side.

He accompanied her out to her car, saw her seated behind the wheel, then bade her, 'Don't work too late, hmm?'

Like *sleep* would be an option anytime soon.

As she cleared the gates she slotted in a CD, turned the dial up loud, and let the sound drown out any coherent thought.

It was only as she entered Marine Parade that she muted the music, and inside the apartment she collected her satchel, bade her father 'goodnight', and went to her room…to work way past midnight before she discarded her clothes and crawled wearily into bed. To sleep within seconds of her head touching the pillow.

It seemed only an hour or two when her alarm sounded, and she groaned out loud as she checked the digital display.

Time to rise and shine and face a new day.

The temptation to burrow her head beneath the pillow was uppermost, and for a few seconds she indulged the possibility before tossing aside the bedcovers.

She needed to hit the shower, dress, grab something to eat, then ride the lift down to her car and head for school.

It helped that her father had fresh coffee, cereal and fruit ready, and she expressed her appreciation, demolished the food in record time, then collected her satchel and blew a kiss in his direction.

'I should be home late afternoon.'

Andre inclined his head. 'I'll be ready.'

The question was…would she?

A thought which permeated her mind as she rode the lift down to the basement car park and remained uppermost as she battled peak-hour traffic to the northern suburbs.

It was her wedding day.

A day when most girls indulged in bridal pampering while her mother and attendants fussed and tended her every need, ensuring all the preparations fell into place with minimum hassle. The dress, the cake, the limousines, the church, reception, food, guests…

Supposedly the best day in a girl's life.

Hah…so much for tradition!

CHAPTER FIVE

TEACHING teenage students could at best be described as a mixed bag, for among the good days were the not-so-good days when everything went to hell in a handbasket.

Today was fast proving to be one of the latter, Romy decided as she marshalled her reserves of strength, tamped down her irritation, and attempted to put an enthusiastic spin on the lesson.

Was it a phase of the moon, the constraints of students being confined indoors on a beautiful early summer's day…or had the class heckling risen by several notches?

Maybe she was just tired and stressed…*whatever,* she just wanted the day to be over.

Although, contrarily, that would only bring her closer to tying the marital knot with Xavier. An event which held certain connotations she was reluctant to explore.

Oh…move right along, why don't you? she urged in silent castigation. It's not as if you haven't slept with him and shared his life…albeit for a few brief months.

So what was the big deal?

Because, a little imp taunted. He was too much, way too much *then*…so what makes you think you can handle him now?

He possessed the power to take hold of her vulnerable emotions and turn them upside down, making her *his* in a way no other man ever could. Even remembering the touch of his hands, his mouth…the passion, delicious, evocative on occasion, wild, primitive…shattering.

Crazy, she thought shakily.

It was a relief when the electronic buzzer signalled the end of class and close of the school day.

Romy gathered up her paperwork and ensured her classroom was clear, then she bypassed the general exodus of students and made her way into the conference room where the principal had called a staff meeting.

Thirty minutes, tops…except the meeting ran on for an hour, and consequently it was after five by the time she reached St Kilda. She took a moment to send Xavier a brief text message as she rode the lift to her apartment.

'I was beginning to worry about you,' Andre greeted her as she walked through the door, and she offered an expressive eye roll.

'Don't ask. I'm on it.'

And she was, taking a record three-minute shower, then, towelled dry, she dressed, tended to her hair, make-up, slipped her feet into stilettos, tossed a few necessities into a carry-bag, then she entered the lounge.

'You're sure about this?'

She'd never been less sure of anything in her life! Except she wasn't about to make that admission. Instead she summoned a smile.

'We need to leave.' An obvious statement if ever there was one. Even if the deity was on her side, it was unlikely they'd reach Xavier's Brighton home before six-thirty.

'You have my love, always,' Andre said quietly as they rode the lift down to the foyer. 'I want you to know that.'

Romy's eyes misted, and she blinked rapidly. 'Likewise.' She couldn't, *wouldn't* let a tear fall. For if perchance one did spill, she'd never be able to stop.

Go with the prosaic, she urged silently. 'I've given you a spare set of keys. If there's any problem, call me and report the problem to maintenance.' She did a mental check and came up with—'I'll stop by Monday after school and collect the rest of my stuff.'

She kept the Mini five kilometres over the speed limit and sent out a silent prayer that no police scanners were active in the vicinity!

The gates guarding the entrance to Xavier's home were open, and she cleared the driveway and slid to a halt in front of two four-wheel-drive vehicles.

Romy was within a metre of the front entrance when the door opened, and Xavier stood in the aperture.

Tall, his broad frame immaculately clothed in expensive tailoring, he presented a compelling figure whose facial expression was impossible to discern.

She felt the need to apologize, but somehow it seemed superfluous, and she made an attempt at humour to defuse the situation.

'It's a bride's prerogative to be late for her wedding,' she offered lightly.

For a brief second she thought she glimpsed a faint gleam of humour in those dark eyes, then it was gone as he acknowledged her father.

Two guests…if *guest* was the appropriate term for Xavier's lawyer and a mature woman introduced as the celebrant, occupied the formal lounge.

A small table draped in white damask and lace held a votive candle, a delicate spray of white orchids, and an ornate leather-bound folder.

Romy felt her insides curl with a mixture of apprehensive fatalism as Xavier moved to her side as polite conversation ensued.

It felt as if she was a disembodied spectator as she smiled, chatted, and attempted to portray the part of a happy bride-to-be.

When in reality her nerves were as taut as finely stretched wire.

Just hold it together, she urged in silent desperation. Three years ago you'd have married Xavier in a heartbeat.

Except that had been then, not now.

'We'll begin, shall we?' the celebrant suggested warmly and indicated where she wanted each of them to stand.

It hardly seemed real, Romy decided as Xavier took both her hands in his, and she stilled the faint shiver threatening to feather the length of her spine.

The words washed over her, and when prompted, she repeated her vows, heard Xavier intone his own, and her hand trembled as he slid a wide diamond-encrusted band on her finger. Seconds later she watched in silent apprehension as he handed her a gold band and extended his left hand, followed soon after by the celebrant's words, 'It gives me pleasure to pronounce you husband and wife.'

Romy's eyes widened as Xavier pulled her close and covered her mouth with his own in a lingering, evocative kiss.

Oh, my…what was that? An expected gesture for those present?

She managed a winsome smile as congratulations were offered, flutes filled with champagne and their health and happiness toasted. Maria served canapés, and Romy accepted the obligatory one, then politely declined anything further, aware there was every possibility her stomach might revolt.

Xavier was *there,* at her side as if joined at the hip…his smile warm as he rested light fingers at the edge of her waist. There was the occasional trail of his hand across her shoulder blades and the moment when he linked his fingers through her own.

Feigned togetherness, she rationalized, sure he was merely playing an expected part…but for whose benefit? Andre knew the truth, and she doubted Xavier's lawyer or the celebrant were overly interested in the *real* reason for the marriage.

Just go with the flow, she silently bade herself. Smile, *pretend* for a little while…where was the harm?

Xavier knew…of course he did. Although it was likely she was the only one who glimpsed the faint amusement apparent, the slight quirk at the edge of his lips.

'Enjoying yourself?' he murmured as he trailed gentle fingers down her cheek.

'Yes.' Her eyes sparkled wickedly. 'This is so—' she paused deliberately '—fun.'

'Isn't it, though?'

Just—*don't kiss me again.* The words didn't find voice, but his eyes gleamed a little as if he'd sensed the silent admonition.

'Bothered you, did it?'

Romy offered him a sweet smile. 'Of course not.'

'Will you be so brave a few hours from now?'

'Without an audience? Bank on it.'

Andre joined them, and the light bantering took a new direction as the merits of Australian sparkling wine were compared with finest French vintage. Any subject, Romy perceived, which didn't touch on the wedding itself.

The celebrant took her leave, whereupon Maria served a tempting three-course meal comprising chicken soup, a delicious paella, followed by a delicate sorbet, after which they adjourned to the lounge for coffee.

All too soon the lawyer declared a need to conclude the evening…a decision which prompted Andre to call for a taxi.

'I'll phone you Monday afternoon,' Romy promised as she hugged her father and saw his answering smile. Then the taxi was there, and she stepped back into the foyer as the rear tail lights disappeared through the gates.

It was impossible to still the faint curling sensation in her stomach as she met Xavier's watchful expression.

She strove for polite. 'What time do you want to leave?'

'As soon as you've packed what you need for the weekend,' he responded with indolent ease, noting the fast-beating pulse at the base of her throat.

She managed a smile. 'It won't take long.' She turned and forced herself to cross the foyer and step lightly up the staircase, aware he ascended at her side.

Did he intend to change his dark suit for more casual wear? She certainly intended to lose the killer heels, and jeans, camisole and jacket would be more comfortable than a dress.

The master bedroom was incredibly spacious, with a large double *en suite* and walk-in robes, a king-size bed, a recessed alcove housing two comfortable chairs, a small table and lamp.

The decor bore a pleasing mix of ivory, varying shades of taupe, highlighted in both *en suites* with marble tiles.

Xavier indicated one of the walk-in robes. 'Maria unpacked your belongings.'

He shrugged off his jacket, loosened and removed his tie, then began unbuttoning his shirt.

OK, this was where she ditched her stilettos and made

for the walk-in robe. And no, she assured herself mentally, it wasn't *escape* as such…merely a need to effect a change of clothes and retrieve a selection to pack. After which she'd move on to the *en suite* and freshen up.

As a plan it worked just fine, although she wasn't quite so fine with Xavier's close proximity. He'd exchanged the formal suit for casual jeans, a chambray shirt and a fashionable leather jacket, and she stifled a silent sigh of relief as he collected both overnight bags and indicated she should precede him from the room.

Did he guess the state of her nerves? Possibly. She had a vivid memory of his intuitive skill at divining her thoughts.

The Mornington Peninsula lay an hour's drive to the south of the city, a route relatively picturesque by day, but providing a different perspective when shrouded by night's darkness.

Xavier slid a CD into the slot as the city's environs became less dense, and Romy leant her head against the cushioned rest, closed her eyes, and let the music seep through to her bones.

She hadn't wanted meaningless conversation…just a welcome silence in which to relax and unwind in order to face whatever the night would bring. Not that she felt in the least inclined to *relax*…

Yet the soft music, the faint motion of the car, combined with anxiety, stress and sleepless nights, took their toll, and she woke to the light stroke of gentle fingers at the edge of her jaw.

For a moment she experienced no sense of time or place. There was only Xavier, leaning close, his eyes dark in the reflected light, and on the edge of that wondrous place between dreamy sleep and wakefulness her lips parted in a soft smile. 'Hi.'

There was the temptation to take her mouth with his own, to taste and savour the sweetness…and encourage her response.

He could, easily. And he almost did, except it would inevitably break the spell, realization would be swift, and she'd resist with spirited dissent.

When he took her, he wanted her awake, aware…and willing.

'We're here.'

Romy's eyes widened as she became conscious of where she was and with whom, and his eyes narrowed slightly as he witnessed her veil her emotions.

He released her seatbelt, then tended to his own before slipping out from behind the wheel, aware she followed his actions.

Check-in was achieved with smooth efficiency, a porter led the way to their suite, performed the obligatory spiel, then left.

Romy spared a brief glance at the large bed and felt her knees go weak at the thought of sharing it with Xavier.

Ridiculous, given she'd been his lover for three beautiful months, and there was no need for first-night nerves or awkwardness.

Sure, and who do you think you're kidding? a small voice taunted as she began unpacking her bag.

It was the *knowing* that was so unsettling. The revival of memories so incredibly intimate, it hurt to recall their existence.

She didn't want to become lost in him…dammit, losing herself wasn't something she could afford. Not if she wanted to retain her emotional sanity.

So she'd have sex with him. Enjoy the physical act and not allow her mind to engage. How difficult could it be?

'Would you like something to drink?'

Romy lifted her head and spared him an enquiring glance. 'As in?'

'Coffee, tea or—'

'You?'

The corners of his mouth lifted in a humorless smile. 'That, too…eventually. Meantime, we could wander along to the lounge bar, sit awhile—'

'And play pretend honeymooners?'

'Then catch an early night.'

She detected the silky tone in his voice and chose to ignore it. The dangerous quality apparent had moved up a notch, and she managed to control the faint shiver threatening to scud down her spine.

Give it up. You're playing with fire.

She collected her toilet bag and set it in the adjoining en suite before re-emerging into the bedroom. 'You mentioned the lounge bar.'

'Wise.'

She wasn't sure delaying the inevitable was such a good idea, for she felt akin to prey waiting for the predator to strike.

It was a luxe resort with beautiful fittings, the lounge bar spacious with exotic planters on display, Romy noted. There were two other couples occupying comfortable chairs grouped at a round table, and Romy offered a faint smile as she crossed to a distant table.

A waitress appeared as soon as they were seated, and it was easy to lean back against the cushions.

'This is a nice place.' It was an ideal setting, even for guests who might choose not to play golf.

'I thought you'd like it.'

So he'd been here before. Undoubtedly with a female

companion. Not, Romy fervently hoped, occupying the same suite. The mere thought verged towards…tacky.

'No,' Xavier offered with indolent amusement, and she arched a deliberate eyebrow.

'As if I care.' Except she did, and it bothered her more than she wanted to admit.

Three *years,* she decried silently? Of course he's been with other women. *Many*…so what if he hadn't brought one of them *here.* Big deal.

The waitress delivered their tea, enquired if they wanted anything else, and when they declined she merely offered a polite smile, took note of their suite number and returned to the bar.

'Is this where we discuss the state of the nation, world economics, your latest take-over venture?' Romy posed, and saw his mouth widen with humour.

'The short or long version?'

'Whatever, as long as you don't send me to sleep.'

'We could, of course, discuss your day.'

'Preferably not.'

'Problems?'

Nothing specific. Just a faint niggle that wouldn't go away. 'It takes a while for a new teacher to be accepted into the student demographic.'

Xavier caught the edge of tiredness in her voice, the pale features and the smudges beneath her eyes which the brief nap during the drive had done little to alleviate.

He stood to his feet. 'Let's go.'

For a brief moment he glimpsed her uncertainty, then it was gone. 'I'm fine.'

Doubtful, he perceived, ignoring her protest.

Her nervous tension rachetted up a few notches as they entered their suite, and she removed her earrings, slid off her watch and bracelet, then she gathered up a cotton sleep-shirt and disappeared into the *en suite,* where she undressed, removed her make-up and cleaned her teeth.

Hardly a pretty sight, she admitted as she spared her mirrored image a glance, and told herself she was beyond caring.

She closed her eyes, then opened them again.

Time to go face her husband…and whatever the night would bring.

Except he wasn't occupying the bed. Nor had he discarded his clothes. Instead, he was seated at the small desk in front of an open laptop.

He glanced up and met the faint surprise evident in her startled gaze. 'Go to bed. I won't be long.'

'You're offering me a reprieve?'

His eyes darkened. 'You want me to change my mind?'

Don't *say* a word, she bade herself silently. Just slip beneath the sheets of the comfortable large bed, settle in, close your eyes, and sleep *if you can.*

She wouldn't, of course. She was too supremely conscious of him sharing the same room…the same bed.

Except the lightly scented sheets, the luxury pillow, were the last things she remembered, and she was unaware Xavier caught her swift passage into somnolence…or that she failed to stir when he slid in beside her from the opposite side of the bed.

Romy woke to the aroma of fresh coffee, and she stretched, unaware of where she was for a few seconds, until recognition dawned, and with it came the need to determine whether she was alone in the bed.

'Breakfast has just arrived.'

Xavier caught her startled glance and took in her tumbled hair, the sleep-shirt which dipped low over one shoulder, saw the moment she realized and quickly lifted a hand to set it in order.

'You slept well.'

Had she? It was obvious from the tossed-back covers that she hadn't slept alone. Had they…? Surely she'd have known. Which brought the question—

'No.'

Pink flooded her cheeks, and she rolled her eyes in self-castigation.

He looked refreshed, attired in chinos and a chambray shirt, trainers on his feet. *Relaxed.* How did he *do* that?

She was suddenly conscious of her rumpled state, a need for the bathroom.

'It's not as if I haven't seen you in a state of undress,' he opined with musing indolence, and she picked up a pillow and heaved it in his direction.

'You could at least afford me some privacy.'

'If you want to play…'

Romy escaped and felt the colour tinge her cheeks as she heard his soft chuckle.

She ran the shower, used the complimentary shampoo on her hair, and took her time before shrugging into a tow-elling robe several sizes too big for her before emerging into the bedroom.

'I've ordered another breakfast to be sent in.'

She crossed to the table and lifted a cover from a plate, saw there was more food than she could cope with, and shook her head. 'There's enough here.' She took a seat and picked up a piece of crisp bacon, munched on it, then sliced a knife through eggs benedict. She poured fresh coffee into her cup, added sugar, and carried cup and saucer to the table.

'I think I might go horse riding while you play golf,' Romy remarked as she perused the brochure.

'What gives you the impression I intend to play golf?' Xavier drawled as he replaced the phone after cancelling the second breakfast order.

She spared him a direct look. 'Maybe because there are two eighteen-hole golf courses?'

He arched an eyebrow. 'Why would I choose to leave my wife alone for the day?'

'Then what do you suggest?'

'Alternatively, we could stay in.'

No need to guess how he proposed they occupy their time. 'Let's not,' she managed evenly as she pushed her plate to one side, her appetite gone.

He wore the tycoon image well, for there was a wealth of power evident in his compelling features. Yet beneath the surface lay the ruthless force of a man who'd fought hard to build a fortune. Someone only a fool would seek to cross.

At the height of their relationship, she wouldn't have had any hesitation in nestling onto his lap and wrapping her arms round his neck as she sought his mouth with her own. Exulting in his response and where it led as they delighted in pleasuring each other until only sexual possession would suffice. Nights that never seemed long enough…and days which passed far too slowly.

Would they ever reach that place again?

Somehow she doubted it.

Yet there was a part of her that longed for the affection he'd accorded her…the laughter, the hope he might offer her more.

'Why don't you go dress,' Xavier suggested. 'We'll drive to Sorrento, explore, have lunch, then go on to Portsea.'

The togetherness thing sounded fine, as long as it didn't feature the bedroom, and she drained the rest of her coffee, then gathered up jeans, a light knitted jumper, fresh underwear, and disappeared into the *en suite* to change.

Contrary to Romy's expectation, they enjoyed a pleasant day exploring the Sorrento boutiques, the galleries, bypassing hotel fare for a leisurely lunch at one of the sidewalk cafés. There were several specialist shops which drew her attention, and she browsed at will, examining the various wares on display.

Xavier rarely left her side, and she was supremely conscious of him, the occasional light touch of his hand at her waist as he directed her attention.

It reminded her of a previous time when she'd imagined he was her world and the entire universe combined. How *naive* had she been? Believing marriage to Xavier to be her ultimate goal.

Conversely, it had become a reality…for all the wrong reasons. Worse, she was at war with her emotions. How was it possible to hate him for making her compliance the pivotal condition in her father's financial rescue package…yet ache with longing to recapture the intimate joy they'd once shared.

Crazy. Like the latter would happen anytime soon…if ever.

And what of her divorce pact?

'You're thinking too much.' Xavier's slightly accented drawl brought forth a brilliant faux smile.

'And you know this…*because?*'

He pressed a light finger to the centre of her lower lip where she'd unconsciously captured the soft inner tissue between her teeth. 'A dead giveaway.'

So much for the cool calm facade!

'Would you prefer to dine here, or return to the resort?'

'You're offering me the choice?'

'That surprises you?'

'Yes,' she relayed sweetly. 'But for the record, let's have dinner here.'

The corners of his mouth tilted with humour. 'Delaying the togetherness thing?'

She didn't pretend to misunderstand. 'How did you guess?'

CHAPTER SIX

THEY enjoyed a leisurely meal in a delightful restaurant where fine food and good wine made for a pleasant evening.

Perhaps it was the goblet of wine which promoted a relaxed almost mellow mood, for it became easy for Romy to relay a few amusing anecdotes.

'Lulubelle as a name might have sounded cute in Grade one,' she reminisced with an impish smile. 'But in Grade ten…it was an accident waiting to happen.'

Xavier leaned back in his chair with the indolence of a man at ease. 'So what did she end up with?'

'Lu or Belle would have been OK, but Lube? Teenagers can be so mean.'

'Eventually she would leave the scholastic system and set a precedent for whichever derivation she preferred.'

'Agreed.' Somehow she doubted anyone had dared shorten his name. 'What about you?'

'No.'

She arched an eyebrow. 'You didn't acquire a nickname?'

He had…a rude generic nickname he'd refused to tolerate, and he'd chosen to enforce his objection physically. A choice that had landed him in the principal's office on a few occasions and brought him within a hair's breadth of expulsion.

'My past is well documented.'

'Bad boy made good with a stellar rise to riches,' she relayed with a tinge of cynical humour. 'With little revelation about the bad stuff.' He had the physical scars to prove just how close he'd come to the edge and she'd seen them, traced a gentle finger and touched her lips to each of them. And regarded him in silent incredulity when he'd downplayed the how, where and why.

A time when she'd wanted to discover who he was beneath the sophisticated facade, to learn his deepest secrets and be *the* one in whom he'd confide.

Except he'd made the journey alone and proved he didn't need anyone. A lone warrior intent on shaping his own destiny.

That he'd succeeded was media legend.

Romy lapsed into silence as the car covered the distance to their resort, and it was after eleven when they entered their suite.

It had been a pleasant day, and she said as much as she removed her jacket and toed off her shoes.

When she turned, he was there, and her eyes widened as he captured her head between his hands and covered her mouth with his own.

Gently, so gently it didn't occur to her to deny him as his tongue explored the soft fullness, tasted, then began an erotic invasion that brought alive her wary emotions and sent them soaring.

She tried to tell herself she didn't want this, except she had no control over the sensations he evoked. No will to protest as his hand cupped her nape while the other slid down her back to lock her close against him.

His arousal was a potent force, and her body quivered

as he slid a hand beneath her jumper, caressed her skin, then slid up to cover her breast.

A silent gasp rose and died in her throat as he stroked the tender peak until it hardened beneath his touch, and she arched in against him and lifted her arms high as they sought purchase at his nape.

It wasn't enough, not nearly enough, and she made no protest as his hands caught the hem of her jumper and lifted it free, then he discarded her bra with equal ease.

'Xavier.' His name was little more than a faint groan as it emerged from her throat, and he brushed his lips against her own.

'No words,' he bade her quietly. 'Just feel.'

And she did, giving in to the rapture pulsating through her body as it invaded every vein, each sensual crevice, until she became lost. His, so totally *his,* she barely sensed the removal of her clothes, and his, until he slid an arm beneath her knees and carried her to the bed.

In one quick movement he dispensed with the bedcovers and drew her down onto the scented sheets.

A generous lover, he took his time exploring each and every erogenous pleasure pulse, teasing with his fingers, his lips, until her body sang from his touch.

It was more than she could bear, and she whimpered as she hovered on the brink, unaware the guttural cries begging for his possession came from her own lips.

Then he was there, his mouth covering her own as he eased his length deep inside, felt her close around him, then he began to move, slowly at first until she joined his rhythm, spiralling high, so high it was all she could do to simply hold on as he tipped her over the edge…then he held her as she fell.

Her heartbeat seemed off the Richter scale, and there

wasn't a word she was capable of voicing. As to moving, she doubted there was a muscle in her body that would respond to any command, mental or physical.

She felt his lips brush her own, then settle in the sweet hollow at the edge of her neck, and the breath hitched in her throat as he trailed his lips over her collarbone and traced a pattern over the gentle swell of her breast.

A faint groan emerged as a husky whisper as he sought a tender peak and suckled, teasing with his teeth before transferring his attention to render a similar salutation to its twin.

She moved restlessly beneath his touch, felt him swell and harden deep inside her as he began to move with such infinite slowness, it took all her control not to urge him into a quicker pace.

Then she felt the sensation build, bringing every sensual nerve into pulsating life.

Oh, my god.

She became a shameless wanton beneath his primitive touch. *His.*

A slave to the sensual magic only he could gift her. Moisture welled in her eyes and spilled to run slowly across the top of each cheekbone and become lost in her hair.

Xavier brushed his lips to her own, savoured them gently, then he carefully released her and drew her trembling body close in against his own.

It was only on the edge of sleep that she realized what they'd shared had been all about her…*her* pleasure, her orgasmic release. She pressed her lips to his chest in silent gratitude and felt his arms tighten fractionally around her slender form.

* * *

Romy woke to the sound of the shower running, and she burrowed her head beneath the pillow for a few minutes before emerging to check the time.

Nine. She hadn't slept this late since for ever…even at weekends.

Naked, she discovered, beneath the bedcovers. A recollection as to *why* intruded as she experienced a vivid recall of the night, the sex…and how it had impacted on her senses. Her body, she added, as each movement provided an avid reminder of tender skin and the pull of little-used muscles.

Dear heaven. A faint groan of despair whispered from her lips. So much for remaining cool and unaffected! Sex sans emotional engagement…with Xavier?

What planet did she think she was on!

In the background she became aware the running water in the shower had ceased, and she hurriedly cast aside the sheet, collected the first thing that came to hand which, she discovered, was Xavier's shirt, and quickly dragged it on.

It was huge: the rear hemline fell below her knees, and she could have wrapped the front edges twice round her slender frame.

Her hair was a tumbled mess, and she finger-forked it back from her face as Xavier emerged from the bathroom, a towel hitched at his hips, and looking far too ruggedly attractive for his own good.

No man she had ever met projected quite such a degree of raw sexuality. Primal heat lay just beneath the surface…an innate knowledge of what it took to gift women sexual pleasure.

He reminded her of a jungle predator in its prime… honed musculature, the tread of a cat, and the heart of a warrior.

'Are you done?'

His light, teasing drawl jerked her back to the present, and warm colour tinged her cheeks.

Three years ago, she'd have laughed with delight, crossed to his side and pulled his head down to her own for a lingering kiss.

Now she felt vaguely defensive, even slightly awkward, which was crazy, and she hugged her arms tightly together beneath her breasts as he crossed to her side.

He touched a light finger to the pulse beating at the base of her throat and slid his hand to cup her cheek.

'My shirt provides an interesting look.' A smile widened his generous mouth as he traced a thumb-pad down to the corner of her lips. He lowered his head and brushed a fleeting kiss to her forehead. 'You should have shared my shower.'

'I don't think so.'

Did she have any idea how defenseless she appeared?

There was a part of him that wanted to take her back to bed…to enjoy again what they'd experienced through the night. But it could wait.

'Pity.'

He was amused, dammit, and she stepped back from him, gathered up clean clothes, then escaped into the bathrooom.

Beneath the pulsing water she closed her eyes against his image. If last night had proved anything, it was that there could be no going back. To fight against him would be an exercise in futility.

Romy made liberal use of the rose-scented soap, then took her time rinsing off.

How difficult could it be to immerse herself in work during the day, and enjoy the benefits of good sex at night?

It was just a matter of emotional survival…hers.

With determined resolve she closed the water dial, reached for a towel and began drying off.

Ten minutes later she emerged into the bedroom attired in linen trousers and a V-necked jumper, her hair twisted into a knot atop her head, wearing minimal make-up and wedge-heeled sandals.

Xavier glanced up from his laptop. 'Do you want to order breakfast in, or shall we eat in the dining room?'

'Dining room,' Romy stated without hesitation and watched as he pressed *save* and closed down.

She was hungry from all that expended energy, she decided ruefully as she tucked into fresh juice, strong black coffee and a cooked meal.

'Brunch,' she said when, almost replete, she bit into toast spread with marmalade.

He refilled his cup with coffee, then leaned well back in his chair. 'We'll check out, then drive further down the coast to Portsea for the day.'

She looked at him carefully. 'I'm fine if you want to head back to Melbourne.' She couldn't, wouldn't call his Brighton mansion *home*. 'I have class papers to mark and lessons to set for tomorrow.' She paused imperceptibly. 'Doubtless you have data you need to check.'

'Nothing that can't wait until evening.'

It was almost midday when they hit the road, and they spent time checking the craft market, where Romy discovered a beautiful multi-coloured beaded bracelet. It was gorgeous, and she happily paid and tucked the tissue-wrapped purchase into her purse.

'You're not going to wear it?'

She spared Xavier a glance as they moved towards the next stall. 'It's a gift.' For a friend, for whom it would be perfect.

Kassi, a dear extrovert whose delicious sense of humour had served to lighten their long study hours during university. A friendship they'd maintained wherever they each happened to be in the world.

Coincidentally, Kassi was now based in Melbourne, teaching at an exclusive private school, and although they'd spoken via phone and met briefly for coffee, so far there hadn't been the opportunity for any in-depth catch-up. Something they'd each vowed to correct over dinner midweek. *Show and tell,* Kassi had said with husky laughter.

Romy tamped down a strangled sound at the thought of explaining her sudden marriage to none other than Xavier DeVasquez.

'You said something?'

She met his speculative gaze and proffered a sweet smile. 'Just clearing my throat.'

His eyes gleamed with sudden humour, almost as if he'd divined her train of thought. Unlikely, she rationalized.

'Do you see anything else you like?' he queried mildly.

Some pretty hand-crafted earrings, dainty and a perfect match for the delicate embroidery on a favourite blouse, except they were beyond her price range, and she simply shook her head and wandered to the next stall with its display of glazed pottery.

His close proximity caused the nerves in her stomach to flutter into disturbing life, and it was all she could do to prevent the faint hitch in her breath as he curved a hand round her shoulder.

You don't *like* him, she reminded herself, and you *hate* that he's using you as a form of blackmail. Yet last night she'd fought a mental battle in his bed, determined not to succumb to his touch…to merely disengage her emotions and refrain from anything other than minimal participation.

So much for any resolution in that department!

All it had taken was the sweep of his mouth on her own, the exploratory tracery of his fingers as he teased each erotic pleasure pulse and brought them achingly alive. Skilfully led her on a seductive path to a place where her mind was no longer her own...and her body became his to command and enthrall.

It wasn't fair. She needed to survive. *Had* to...or she'd never emerge from the relationship with her emotions intact.

Some chance! Only two days into the marriage, and she was already at odds with herself...emotionally, mentally, physically.

Go with the flow and enjoy the ride, a devilish little imp taunted. Milk it with all you've got.

Sure, and she could do that. She was no sycophant, and she refused to become one. So where did that leave her?

Precisely where she was...in a permanent state of un-enviable ambivalence.

It was late afternoon when Xavier took the Nepean Highway north to Brighton. As they neared the city he diverted to a small Italian restaurant where they dined on a divine salad, followed by pasta, and settled for coffee before continuing the few kilometres to his Brighton mansion.

Xavier took their bags upstairs to the master suite, and Romy joined him, unpacked, and then she gathered up her laptop and satchel.

'You can use my home office.'

Sharing a space with him wasn't conducive to clarity of focus, and she indicated the alcove. 'Thanks, but I'll be fine here.'

She didn't see the musing gleam in his dark eyes as she crossed the room and took time gathering together every-thing she needed.

When she glanced up scant minutes later, he had already exited the room, and she set to work. With two morning and two afternoon classes in different grades, she needed to ensure the appropriate texts were flagged and various notations made.

Next came the assignments that required marking, and she lined the papers up, then began, notebook to one side and red pen in hand.

It took a while, and she was half done when she came across a loose sheet of folded paper. Had it been inadvertently added to the assignments by mistake?

An unsigned computer print-out comprising a few lines, and at first glance it seemed innocuous, just a long sentence outlining praise for her dedication as a teacher. She refolded the paper and slid it into the sleeve of her satchel.

It was late when she packed up. She showered and then, moving into the bedroom, she viewed the large bed, undecided which side she should choose.

'Does it matter?'

She heard Xavier's slightly amused drawl and uttered a startled sound as she turned to face him.

She hadn't heard him enter the room, and her eyes clashed with his own for a few timeless seconds until he began freeing the buttons on his shirt.

An action which galvanized her into mobility, and she quickly moved to the bed, slid between the sheets and pulled the covers up to her chin, studiously choosing to look anywhere but at the man who unselfconsciously stripped off his clothes and walked naked into the *en suite*.

Sleep should have come easily, except every muscle in her body seemed tense, and she shifted position twice before curling onto her side.

Romy heard him re-enter the room, sensed him slide

beneath the covers on the opposite side of the bed, and then heard the almost undetectable click as the room was plunged into darkness.

For endless minutes she silently recited Byron, then she switched to counting numbers…reaching one hundred before conducting a mental run-through of passive verbs.

Nothing seemed to work, and she consciously slowed her breathing, reflected on memories from happier times, only to give a startled cry as she sensed a faint movement, then strong arms gathered her close.

'*Mierda.*' The husky oath sounded close to her ear. 'Relax.'

Like she could do that curved in against his naked body, with his warm palm cupping her breast and one long muscular leg looped over her legs?

'Sleep…unless you want me to help you with that?'

'No. Please—' Her voice was little more than an indistinct choking sound.

His warm breath fanned softly over her head, and she could feel the solid beat of his heart against her back. It felt…good, and her own heartbeat slowed, then her eyelids drifted down as she slipped into a dreamless state.

When she woke, the early morning light was filtering into the room, and she turned, saw the bed was empty, and she picked up her watch to check the time.

There was no sign of Xavier as she quickly selected fresh underwear and outer clothes. Showered and dressed, her hair swept into a smooth knot atop her head, minimal make-up in place, she caught up her laptop and satchel and made her way downstairs to the kitchen where the aroma of freshly made coffee smelt wonderful.

Xavier was seated at the table in the adjoining informal breakfast room, and his piercing gaze speared her own for a few seconds. 'Good morning.'

She had no reason to feel slightly awkward, and she covered it well by offering a sunny smile. 'Hi.'

He looked the quintessential business tycoon, freshly shaven, well-groomed, and attired in a three-piece designer suit, undoubtedly crafted especially for him.

At this hour of the morning he was too much. Oh, why not tell it how it was…Xavier is too much at *any* hour of the day or night!

Maria bustled in from the kitchen bearing freshly made toast and cereal. 'It's a lovely morning,' she greeted warmly. 'I hope you slept well?'

It was a polite, rhetorical query. Yet recalling *how* she'd slept, curled up against Xavier's naked form, brought a faint tinge of pink to her cheeks, and she managed a polite, 'Very well, thank you.' And deliberately refrained from glancing in his direction as she poured steaming coffee into her cup and added sugar before taking an appreciative sip.

'You have a full day ahead of you?'

Romy selected toast, fresh fruit and yoghurt, and she began preparing both as she answered him. 'Classes back-to-back, with a short afternoon break.' It was only polite to ask, 'And you?'

'Busy. A late meeting which will probably run over time.'

'So don't wait dinner?'

'No.' He checked his watch, then drained the remainder of his coffee and rose to his feet. 'I need to leave.'

She was unprepared for him to cross to her side, capture her chin and possess her mouth in a brief, evocative kiss that succeeded in sending her emotions every which way but loose.

It irked that he knew, and she gave him a speaking glance as he lifted his head. She expected to see mockery evident, but there was none.

What *was* that? Staking a claim, setting a precedent, or merely exerting his powerful ownership?

'Take care.' Without a further word he collected his laptop and briefcase, bade Maria a brief goodbye, then strode from the room.

Romy made a conscious effort to finish her breakfast, but her appetite had disappeared, and she merely refilled her cup with coffee and drank it down; then she gathered her laptop and satchel, acknowledged Maria's presence, and made her way to the garage, fired up her Mini, and battled heavy peak-hour traffic en route to the northern suburbs.

CHAPTER SEVEN

A PHONE call to Kassi during a break from class ensured they set up a time and place to meet Wednesday evening. The fact it coincided with Kassi's birthday was incidental.

Romy entered the restaurant a few minutes early and followed the hovering *maître d'* to a corner table where Kassi was already seated.

'Hey there.' Kassi stood, and they hugged, laughed, then subsided into chairs. 'I ordered champagne to be delivered the instant you arrived.'

Dear Kassi…beautiful, tall, slender, long wavy sable-coloured hair and the most expressive dark eyes any number of women would kill for.

'It's so great to see you,' Romy enthused, and Kassi gave an infectious grin. 'It's been a while.'

'Like…three *years?* We have so much to catch up on.'

E-mail correspondence and phone calls had sufficed, but nothing came close to face-to-face contact.

'First and foremost, let's do the birthday thing!' Romy reached into her purse, extracted the brightly wrapped gift, and presented it together with a card. 'Happy birthday!'

'Do I get to open it now?'

It was easy to smile. 'Of course.'

Kassi read the card and became a little misty-eyed. 'You have a way with words. Thank you.' She dispensed with the paper and the tissue surrounding the gift, then she gave a delighted exclamation as she retrieved the bracelet. 'It's gorgeous.' She slid it on, then she rose to her feet and brushed her lips to Romy's cheek. 'I love it.'

A waiter appeared, proffered the chilled bottle of champagne, received Kassi's approving nod, then he proceeded to pull the cork and fill their flutes.

'Here's to us.' Kassi lifted her flute and lightly pressed the rim to Romy's.

They each took an appreciative sip, savoured the superb French vintage, then regarded each other with the pleasure of a long friendship.

'Are you planning to tell me the significance of the ring you just happen to be wearing on your left hand?' Kassi's eyes sparkled. 'Is it what I think it is?'

She'd seriously given thought to slipping it off and dropping it into her purse before she left the car. Except at the last minute she couldn't do it.

Any day soon news of their marriage would reach the media. How long would it take a savvy reporter to make the *Picard* connection? Hours…a day, at most. It wouldn't take much to do the maths, or for the speculation to begin.

'Yes.'

Kassi shrieked, then laughed, and gave her a warm hug.

'Congratulations! How come you didn't tell me on the phone?' She gave a delighted grin. 'OK, girlfriend…*details. Who* and when…and don't leave out a thing.'

'Early evening on Friday,' Romy began carefully. 'The wedding was very private, just immediate family.'

'Given you've only been home a fortnight, I gather this has been a whirlwind affair? Yes?' Kassi's eyes twinkled with humour. *'Give,* Romy! Who is he? Someone you met while you were away?'

She hesitated for all of a few seconds. 'It's Xavier DeVasquez.'

She saw Kassi's eyes widen, then cloud with concern. 'I think,' her friend managed slowly after a measurable silence, 'you need to explain.'

She owed Kassi the truth…or at least a diluted version of it. For it had been Kassi who'd witnessed her involvement with Xavier. A dear friend who'd cared enough to listen, support and commiserate as Romy had dealt with the break-up.

The waiter presented them each with a menu, and Kassi waved him aside as she fixed Romy with an intent look. 'I take it this isn't a love match?'

'No.' It was nothing less than the truth. Lust, certainly, but not love.

'So there has to be a solid reason why you've gone along with it.' Kassi's features softened. 'Do you want to tell me? In confidence, of course.'

Something Romy could rely on…not that it made it any easier to relay the facts. 'My father owed him a large sum of money.' A simple truth which didn't fool Kassi for a second.

'Xavier, damn his diabolical heart, ruthlessly offered a pay-back scenario…which you failed to throw back in his face *because*…?'

'He had every reason to press charges, and dad would have gone to prison.'

'Oh…*hell.*'

Precisely.

'That's it? All of it?'

Not quite all, but as much as she was prepared to reveal. 'Shall we order?' Romy lifted a hand to summon the waiter. 'I don't know about you,' she said lightly. 'But I'm famished.'

They perused the menu, ordered a starter, a main, and held off on dessert.

Romy lifted her flute and took a small sip, then she viewed Kassi over the rim. 'Your turn to bring me up to date.'

'I have the pampered darlings of the rich and famous who can tell a Manolo Blahnik from a Jimmy Choo at twenty paces,' Kassi offered in faintly droll tones. 'A Collette Dinnigan from Sass & Bide, Prada from Versace. Mention the Paris Collection and they can recite the *who's who* of designers and the models who'll feature them.'

Romy couldn't restrain a grin. 'Ah, the important stuff.'

'Convincing the majority there's importance in the history of the Renaissance, the Arts, and it's a lost cause.'

'Which, to some of the students, it is.'

Kassi rolled her eyes. 'Unless, of course, nepotism runs rife and they coast into mother's gallery, or father's corporation.'

A light chuckle emerged from Romy's throat. 'Let's not forget mother's boutique, or the family firm.'

'There is the exception,' Kassi posed. 'I have a student in the twelfth grade who appears to be determined to make it without any influence from her exceptionally rich parents. The father is a high-flyer, and his daughter intends to follow in his footsteps…in direct competition.'

The waiter delivered their starter, and they ate the decorative morsel in relative silence.

'While you,' Kassi ventured, 'taught teenagers from underprivileged backgrounds in what could be loosely termed a poverty-stricken area where gang fights were the norm.' She paused imperceptibly. 'You rarely mentioned anything untoward. But I imagine there were a few instances you had to contend with over the past three years.'

'Some,' she acknowledged in a non-committal voice as she mentally reflected on the worst of them. The stabbings, bashings, the presence of police on a too frequent basis. Angry parents, the threats of physical violence. Teenagers who knew every angle there was…and how to work it. Old before their time, street-savvy and merely living to survive.

Some managed to gain a scholarship and get out with a chance to do better, make something of themselves. It had become her mission to instil the need to study, to succeed. She wanted to make a difference…and she had, even if the numbers were pitifully few.

'Opposite ends of the scholastic spectrum,' Kassi concluded. 'And now you're back where you belong on home ground. Once again choosing a tough school.' She paused as the waiter presented their main course and didn't continue until he'd retreated. 'Will Xavier allow you to continue teaching?'

'It's not up for negotiation.'

Kassi's eyes lit up with approval. 'Go—*you*.'

It was as they lingered over coffee that Romy posed the question she had yet to ask.

'And you, Kassi,' she ventured quietly. 'Is there a special someone in your life?'

There was a few seconds' pause. 'Wondered when we'd get around to it.' She made a slight *moue*. 'There's someone who'd like to be special.'

Romy's eyes sharpened. *'But?'*

'He refuses to take *not interested* for an answer.'

'Persistent, is he?'

'Very.'

'Not in a nuisance way?' Heaven forbid, not—

'Stalking me? No. He's just *there*. Friendly, warm, fun.'

'So what's the problem?'

'It's me.'

'You're holding back…why?'

'There was a guy, a year ago,' Kassi admitted with a degree of reluctance. 'It isn't a pretty story.' Her eyes darkened and became bleak. 'I'm not ready to trust anyone else…if I'll ever be ready.'

Romy refilled her cup, then took a measured sip. 'Does the current man know any of this?'

'Yes.'

'And?'

Kassi lifted her shoulders in a light shrugging gesture. 'He says he's content to wait…as long as he can be in my life.'

'That bothers you?'

'A little.'

'Ah.'

'Would you care to elaborate on that?'

Romy couldn't help the light laugh that bubbled from her lips. 'Not right now, no.'

The waiter presented their bill, and they paid their share, finished their coffee, and walked out together to their cars.

Kassi leant forward and brushed her cheek to Romy's. 'Let's do this again soon.'

It was almost eleven when Romy garaged the Mini alongside Xavier's Maybach, and she was crossing the lobby when Xavier appeared from his home office.

Her heart quickened to a faster beat at the sight of him. He'd exchanged his formal business suit for casual trousers and a collarless shirt, the sleeves of which were rolled back over each forearm.

He projected a dangerous sexual masculinity, and she felt her insides begin to curl as he offered her a lazy smile.

'Hi.' Her voice didn't sound quite like her own, and she paused as he set the alarm and moved towards her.

'Hi, yourself,' he drawled. 'How was dinner?'

'Fine. We caught up.'

'Good.'

Romy crossed to the staircase, aware he moved at her side as they ascended to the upper level, and she entered their bedroom, shrugged out of her jacket, then slid off her stilettos. A move which left her at a height disadvantage.

It was ridiculous to feel overwhelmed as he began freeing the buttons on his shirt, and when he reached for the belt at his waist, she crossed to the *en suite,* removed her make-up, her clothes, then she donned sleep pants and tank top, caught back her hair, and re-entered the bedroom…to find the light dimmed and Xavier stretched out beneath the bedcovers with his hands crossed behind his head.

There was a part of her that wanted to slide into bed, have him reach out and just hold her. Let her snuggle close within those strong arms, tuck her head into the curve of his shoulder, breathe in the scent of his clean skin, the faint muskiness of man, and feel secure in the knowledge *here* was where she was meant to be.

To fall asleep knowing some time through the night he'd seek her for the loving he did so well. Too well, for she could almost feel the violently sweet sensation encompass her body, ensuring his slightest caress would send fire coursing through her veins.

'Come here.' His voice was a husky sensual drawl, and her eyes widened as he freed one arm and held out his hand.

'It's late,' she managed and saw his mouth curve into a smile.

'And you're tired.' He threaded his fingers through her own as she reached him. 'Headache?' With a slight tug he eased her down beside him and pressed his lips to her temple.

'Just…it's been a long day.'

He'd seen the slight darkness apparent in her eyes, the faint shadows beneath them. 'Want to tell me about it?'

It felt good, better than good to lie curved in against him. It reminded her of other times when they'd lain like this and the cares of the day had dissipated beneath the soothing touch of his hand, his lips.

'Can I take a rain check?'

He shifted position to lean over her as his mouth closed over her own, teasing a little as the tip of his tongue explored hers, easing inside to tantalize at will.

She felt his hands slide to her waist, find the hem of her tank top and slip beneath it to seek the soft contours of each breast, cup them, then caress the tender peaks with his thumbs until they hardened beneath his touch.

'You don't play fair,' Romy groaned as his mouth slid down to the sensitive hollow at the base of her throat.

'Tell me to stop.'

Except it was too late as he slid the tank top high and covered one sensitized peak with his mouth, laving it until she arched up against him. She cried out as he began to suckle, and the breath hitched in her throat as he slid a hand beneath her sleep pants, sought and found her sensitive clitoris and brought it to vibrant pulsating life.

It was almost more than she could bear, and she helped him get rid of her sleep wear, then he was there, entering her in one slow slide, stilling as her inner muscles contracted around him before he began to move.

Slowly at first, almost withdrawing completely before surging in to the hilt, gradually increasing each thrust until she caught and matched his rhythm…and it was she who cried out, she who clung as he held her at the brink, before tipping them both into a gloriously sensual free fall.

This, Romy mused on the edge of sleep, was the one good thing in this marriage. In the dark of night she could almost believe the past and the now were entwined…even though she knew them to be separate entities.

It almost gave her hope for the future…*almost.*

Except in the light of day her perception would change as reality intervened.

CHAPTER EIGHT

IT WAS a beautiful early summer's evening, the sky paling to an opalescent glow as dusk descended. Street lamps sprang alive as Xavier eased the luxury Mercedes through the wide tree-lined streets towards the city hotel where the night's charity event was being held.

It'll be fine, Romy assured herself silently as she attempted to still the fluttering nerves in her stomach. You've attended a few of these events with Xavier in the past. There'll be several guests whom you've met before…familiar names forming part of the city's social elite.

The Collette Dinnigan gown complimented her colouring and petite stature with its floaty style and gorgeous mix of aqua and varied shades of blue. Strappy stilettos lent added height, and the diamond earrings and matching pendant provided understated *class*.

To aid a sophisticated image, she'd swept her hair into an elaborate twist and secured it with a stylish comb. Carefully applied make-up appeared minimal with emphasis on her eyes and a touch of blusher to her cheeks. Soft colour emphasized the curve of her mouth.

Five hours, Romy reminded herself, where she'd smile,

make conversation, sip excellent wine and nibble on designer food.

How difficult could it be?

'You have no need to be nervous.'

The sound of Xavier's faintly accented drawl brought a wry smile to her lips.

'Sure,' she said. 'And cows jump over the moon.'

His husky chuckle curled round her nerves and tugged a little. 'We've done this before, if you recall.'

'*Before* being the operative term.' A time when she'd imagined herself to be gloriously in love with the man at her side. Except now the circumstances had changed.

'Relax.'

And she could do that?

Romy merely cast him a telling look, then focused her attention on the scene beyond the windscreen as Xavier entered the traffic lane leading to the hotel entrance.

Cameras, lights, action, she thought silently as a uniformed attendant opened the passenger door and moved to one side in order for her to alight.

She was dimly aware of Xavier moving to her side as an attendant drove the luxury Mercedes down into the underground parking area…and the necessity to *smile* as she braved a camera flash.

Xavier DeVasquez's presence attracted media attention by virtue of his financial position and his known generosity to certain charities.

The fact that Romy accompanied him would cause speculation. The existence of her wedding ring…and his own, would only add to the rumour mill. Inevitably, the connection to Andre Picard's fall from grace would be made, and conjecture would run rife.

So what? Wasn't there an axiom that tabled one should smile in the face of adversity?

So she'd smile until her facial muscles ached, talk the talk as if all was right in her world.

Did Xavier have any idea what it cost her to *pretend?* Perhaps...not that it helped.

The event was being held in the hotel ballroom, and the numerous guests converged in the adjoining lounge where waitstaff served drinks and bite-size canapés.

Men attired in dark evening suits, crisp white linen and black bow tie...a mix of wealthy retirees, captains of industry and the upwardly mobile young scions.

Women in designer gowns, wearing jewellery that would fund a Third World nation, beautifully coiffed, exquisitely made-up...whose main purpose was to schmooze, gossip and, in the case of some, keep an eagle eye on their husbands, should their attention wander.

The reverse also applied, Romy deduced, as she glimpsed one society maven flirt with an attractive man who could have been her son, had she been a child bride.

Xavier's presence garnered interest, heightened by the young woman at his side, and Romy could almost sense the ripple of 'isn't that one of his former mistresses? Romy...*who?* The name's on the tip of my tongue.'

OK, so she'd admit to being sensitive. Who wouldn't be, in a similar circumstance? Yet not so sensitive she'd cut and run.

Suck it up, a tiny imp prompted, and play *pretend.*

'Xavier.' The husky purr was definitely female. 'Darling, do introduce me to your...companion.'

The slight pause was deliberate, and Romy's mouth curved into a teasing smile as the woman looked in silent askance at the man at her side.

'Madeleine,' he acknowledged politely. 'My wife, Romy.' He caught Romy's hand and lifted it to his lips. '*Querida,* Madeleine Forbes-Smythe.'

Oh, my. What woman wouldn't *melt* beneath the deliberately sensual heat apparent in those dark, almost black eyes?

'Wife?'

It was amazing how one simple word could hold such a varying degree of emotion, and Romy managed a deliciously rapt expression as she turned towards Madeleine. 'Yes.' She almost added a trite cliche, then decided against it.

'I had no idea,' the woman managed with credible pleasure. 'I take it the marriage is very recent?'

'A week ago,' Xavier said with an indolent smile.

'I must offer my congratulations. And add how delighted I am for you both.' The smile was almost as fake as Madeleine's beautifully lacquered nails.

'How kind,' Romy acknowledged sweetly. 'Thank you.' She tilted her head and offered Xavier a stunning smile. 'Darling, would you mind fetching me some champagne?'

All he needed to do was signal a hovering waiter, and within seconds she was nursing a frosted flute of sparkling wine.

'Isn't this fun?' She lifted the flute in silent challenge. 'Want to share, darling?'

His eyes held hers as he wrapped his fingers round her own and brought the flute to his lips, savouring its contents slowly, then he lowered his hand and idly released it.

'Do you plan any further sharing?'

'Possibly.' Her eyes assumed a challenging gleam. 'If we're served different meals.'

He leant in close and said quietly, 'Don't forget I get to take you home.'

She sent him a sparkling look. 'Hmm, can't wait.'

His soft laughter sounded close to her ear. 'Is that an invitation?'

'No.'

'Liar.'

She felt his lips brush her temple and tamped down the languorous warmth sweeping through her body. Denying him meant denying herself the passion he managed to arouse with very little effort at all.

It was perhaps as well the ballroom doors opened, and the guests were invited to assume their seats at the numerous reserved tables.

Tickets were presented, directions offered, and Romy was supremely conscious of Xavier's hand at her waist as they made their way to the front of the large room.

Was it her imagination, or were they garnering overt attention? Debatable whether the cause was news of their marriage beginning to spread, or merely curiosity regarding Xavier DeVasquez's latest woman.

Round tables seating ten were soon filled, drink waiters hovered whilst unintrusive background music filtered through speakers, and there was sufficient time to converse before the chairwoman of the charity organization took the podium and presented a speech lauding the amount raised, while encouraging the evening's guests to donate generously to the cause.

Their seating plan featured two couples whom Romy vaguely remembered meeting at a similar function several years ago, a beautiful blonde who openly flirted with her companion whilst sending covert glances in Xavier's direction, and two men in their early forties whom Romy knew to be gay.

The waitstaff began serving starters, and Romy surreptitiously observed the blonde's play for attention.

'Don't let her bother you,' a male voice advised quietly, and she turned slightly to face the young man seated beside her. Robert, she recalled, whose partner, Anthony, was big in interior decorating.

'It's good to see you back with Xavier.'

Wonder if you'd say that if you knew the circumstances? Words she refrained from uttering aloud. 'Thank you,' she said graciously.

There was entertainment throughout the evening, featuring a comedian, a parade of designer wear, and a singer.

The comedian's appearance featured between the starter and the serving of the main course. A skilled raconteur, he was a riot, and had everyone laughing at his anecdotes and jokes. He made it easy for the guests to lighten up, including Romy, who clapped delightedly when he simply stood still and silent on stage for several seconds before falling to his knees begging for applause.

Xavier leant close at one stage during the routine and curved an arm loosely round her waist, and for the space of a few minutes she was conscious only of him, the warmth of physical contact, together with the exclusive scent of his cologne. Aware, on a subliminal level, of his power and sexual appeal...the promise of passion that seeped into her bones and spread throughout her body.

How did he *do* that?

Was he similarly affected?

Oh, *get real,* she admonished silently. It's an act. Except he wasn't the only one who could *act.*

The blonde seated opposite had rachetted up the flirting stakes, to the slight embarrassment of her partner, and Romy placed a hand on Xavier's thigh.

An action which drew his immediate attention, and she met the dark eyes close to her own with equanimity.

'You have an admirer.'

'Andrea?'

'Shall I become all proprietorial and flash my wedding ring?' Romy posed sweetly. 'Or would that be a little too much, do you think?'

'She's merely playing a game.'

'Ah,' she ventured sagely. 'Perhaps I should play, too.' She lifted a hand and trailed light fingers down his cheek…only for him to capture her hand with his own and bring it to his lips.

Her mouth parted as he took the tip of one finger and gently bit it with his teeth. 'Not fair.'

Xavier merely smiled and carried their joined hands down onto his lap. For a wild second she was tempted to move her hand, only for his fingers to tighten on her own.

'Can't take the heat, huh?' she taunted softly, and saw his eyes darken.

'You'll keep.'

The waitstaff came out in force as they moved swiftly to present the main course, and Romy concentrated on the artistically arrayed food.

Models took to the catwalk following the main course, displaying a selection of the latest fashion in evening wear, formal and casual wear. The background music moved up a few beats, strobe lights provided special effects, and there was resounding applause as the last model disappeared backstage.

Dessert followed, then coffee, and it became the time of the evening when guests moved from their reserved seating and caught up with friends.

Soon, Romy perceived with a degree of relief, the night would be over and they could leave.

Except she hadn't factored in just how quickly news of

their marriage had spread, ensuring their passage from the ballroom became stalled as various guests sought to offer their congratulations.

It wasn't difficult to stand at Xavier's side with his hand at her waist and smile. Although the smile almost slipped a fraction when his hand slid low to rest against the curve of her bottom…and stayed there.

If he was intent on making a statement as to their togetherness, that would probably work…the question had to be, for how long.

It seemed inevitable a journalist and photographer from the media should request a formal statement, and Xavier acquiesced with a few brief details.

'I understand you've recently renewed the relationship.'

He spared Romy a deep, passionate look that was wholly primitive. 'Yes.'

Wow…it was all she could do not to melt in a puddle at his feet. Even though she knew it was all for the press.

There was the flash of a camera, and the moment was captured for posterity…undoubtedly set to appear in major Australian newspapers the next day.

'Three years after you broke up.'

Oh, my…facts relayed by a *reliable* source or three, Romy perceived wryly, aware the social rumour mill had sprung into action.

Xavier skilfully brought the interview to a conclusion. 'If you'll excuse us?'

The witching hour of midnight fell as Xavier requested the concierge to summon the Mercedes to the front entrance, and Romy bit back a sigh of relief as Xavier eased the powerful car into the night-time traffic vacating the city.

'That was fun,' Romy said as she spared him a cynical glance as they paused at a set of traffic lights.

'It could have been worse.'

'Really?' The emphasis was deliberate and earned her a darkly quizzical smile. 'Perhaps you'd care to explain the touchy-feely thing happening back there.'

'You found it objectionable?'

No, she hadn't…that was the thing. She'd also restrained the instinctive urge to lean in against him and take pleasure from the moment.

'You'd prefer me to be distant? Neglectful of you?'

Her answer was swift and without reservation. 'Don't you care what people think?'

'No.'

The external lights illuminated the mansion as Xavier used a remote to open the gates and another to activate the garage door as he entered the circular driveway.

Home…not that she regarded it as such, unsure whether she ever could.

There were issues she was unable to foresee being resolved—the worst of which had been Xavier blackmailing her into marriage…an action she'd never forgive.

'We have a marriage,' Xavier reminded her as they entered the house, and she sent him a direct look.

'Your insistence, not mine.'

'You'd be wise to accept the situation.' His voice held a silky element she chose to ignore.

'Or else?'

They began to ascend the stairs. 'You want to fight?' Xavier posed coolly, and she shook her head.

'Not particularly.'

They reached the upper level and turned towards the master suite.

'Then give it up, Romy. It serves no purpose.'

It irked her that he was right, and she slid off her stilettos as they entered the bedroom, removed her jewellery, then she reached for the zip fastening at the back of her dress.

Aware, as she did so, that Xavier had shrugged off his jacket, removed his bow tie and shirt, and was in the process of shedding his trousers.

Without a word she went into the *en suite* and removed her make-up, took out the comb and few pins holding her hair in place, then she reached for her sleep tank top.

'You won't need it.'

She looked up in startled surprise and caught sight of Xavier in the mirror as he moved to stand behind her.

Her eyes darkened and became stormy as she met the slumbrous passion evident in his gaze, and her lips parted in remonstrance as his hands closed over her shoulders. Playing pretend in public was OK, but she couldn't, *wouldn't* carry the pretence into their private life. 'We're alone,' she managed coolly. 'There's no one around to impress.'

He lowered his head, and his mouth sought the sensitive hollow at the edge of her neck. 'Except you.'

Sensation leapt deep inside and began flooding her body, bringing alive every sensory nerve end, and it was all she could do not to groan out loud as his hands slid down her upper arms and curved beneath the soft fullness of her breasts.

Who are you trying to kid? He only has to *touch* you and you become lost. *Pretend?* Forget it…this is *real*.

So real, her whole being became incandescent as myriad sensations invaded every cell, and she was incapable of moving so much as a muscle as he slid a hand down over her stomach.

He held her against him, skin on skin, and she became achingly aware of his arousal, the way he cupped her breast and teased the tender peak into a hard, sensitized nub.

'Xavier—' His name emerged from her lips as a helpless groan, and she cried out as he employed skilful fingers to bring her close to climax.

'Want me to stop?'

She began to convulse as he held her, and she simply shook her head, unable to utter so much as a word.

It was almost more than she could bear, and with one easy movement he lifted and turned her in his arms, sliding his hands down to cup her bottom as he held her high against him.

In automatic reaction she wound her arms round his neck and held on as he touched his lips to her breast, savoured the peak, then took it into his mouth and suckled until she cried out… It was then he slid one hand up to cup her nape as he covered her mouth with his own in a kiss that possessed, plundered, and unleashed a primal hunger so intense there could be only one ending.

Oh, my god…*please.*

And he did, positioning her carefully to accept his length as he slid her down, his eyes spearing her own as he watched those beautiful blue pools darken and coalesce…then it was he who trapped a husky groan deep in his throat as he felt her contract around him, sensed her instinctive need for more…so much *more.*

With care he began to move, guiding her body into a rhythm that met and matched his own, as together they scaled the sensual heights with an unleashed passion that was libidinous, electrifying…*pagan.*

Romy was aware only of the man, the incredible sensation as she clung to him, her breathing almost out of control…holding on because it was beyond her capability to do anything else.

It seemed an age before he carefully disengaged and slid

her down to her feet, one arm curving down her back as he held her against him.

With gentleness he cupped her face, tilting it so she had to look at him.

Eyes, large deep-blue shimmering pools, met his, naked of any pretence...and he bit back an imprecation in his own language.

Por Dios, a man could drown in those eyes.

He lowered his head and brushed his lips to her own, caressing with a feather-light touch until her mouth parted in response to a kiss so incredibly gentle she wanted to cry.

Tears welled, then spilled to run in twin rivulets down her cheeks. A husky groan escaped his throat as he traced each one with his lips, and she gasped as he slid one arm beneath her knees and carried her into the bedroom.

Romy felt the cool sheets beneath her back as he slid into bed with her cradled in his arms, and she murmured indistinctly as he drew up the covers and settled her close against him.

On the edge of sleep a silent voice whispered inside her head...*so much for remaining immune.*

Togetherness was fine, she decided over breakfast, but she felt the need for some space, and what was more, she needed to expand her wardrobe...evening wear, in particular.

Xavier, when told of her plans, raised no objection.

'I need to check through data in preparation for a brief trip to New York.'

Her eyes widened a little. 'When do you leave?'

'Early tomorrow morning.' A slight smiled curved his generous mouth. 'Is that a problem?'

'No, of course not.'

She set off around eleven and didn't return until five, elated she'd managed to score two gowns at sale price.

It was late when she retired to bed, and it was she who took control when he drew her close. She who insisted on setting the pace…who caressed the jagged scar scoring three of his ribs. A keloid scar from unskilled surgery close to his hip. And he bit back a husky groan as she hovered close to his erection and deliberately brushed its silken length with her lips, at the same time she cupped him and squeezed a little.

Then it was she who gasped as he rolled and pinned her beneath him, and he covered her mouth with his own as he entered her in one powerful thrust…his eyes dark as he watched her shatter.

CHAPTER NINE

ROMY stirred at the fleeting touch to her cheek, murmured something indistinct, then rolled onto her stomach and buried her head beneath the pillow.

It was still dark, too early, and she needed to sleep.

There was a vague awareness of Xavier's presence, the soft click of the bedroom door as he left, before she slid back into blissful oblivion.

When she woke, the sun was filtering through the bedroom shutters, and all it took was one glance at the time and she hit the *en suite* running.

Monday. Dammit, it was a school day.

Breakfast didn't happen, and she took a tub of yoghurt, a banana and coffee-to-go, offered Maria a hurried and somewhat wry 'hello'…quickly followed by 'goodbye' as she almost ran to the garage.

It was amazing how much peak-hour traffic build-up there was by leaving fifteen minutes later than her normal schedule. If there could be a plus side, it provided the opportunity to snack on her breakfast-to-go at the numerous enforced stops at various traffic-controlled intersections en route to the northern suburbs.

Her arrival in the school grounds coincided with the

buzzer announcing commencement of the first morning class. A morning which thankfully progressed in a reasonably uneventful manner.

There was little time to reflect on the previous night or the mesmerizing intensity of Xavier's lovemaking. Sex, she amended. Just…very good sex. Dammit, she was almost willing to swear she could still feel the imprint of his possession. As to her response…it was better she didn't go there. Wild and wanton, the silky purr of her voice…had that been *her?*

Hello, a silent voice taunted. Focus on the prosaic, the here and now of a classroom filled with teenage students who'd take advantage of any opportunity she inadvertently provided.

With determination she directed their attention to the technicalities of pleonasm and the meaning of epigrammatic within written text…and withheld a faint smile at the collective groan of reluctance.

It was during an afternoon break between classes that Romy came across another note among homework assignments handed in during an early morning class.

Once again, she examined every word for any hidden meaning and found none. The only factor that gave concern was the lack of a name…just *a grateful student.* Which meant it could be anyone she taught in English classes.

On impulse she put a call through to Andre and arranged to visit on her way home. It would be good to chat in person, instead of via the phone, and she suggested they share dinner. Even better, she'd stop off at a supermarket, purchase the necessary ingredients and surprise him by preparing their meal.

She also rang Maria and told her not to make dinner.

It was almost five when she used a spare key to enter her apartment.

'Hi. I'm—' she almost said *home,* only to change it at

the last moment to '—here.' She went through to the kitchen and deposited two grocery bags onto the counter, then began unpacking them as Andre entered the room.

'Romy…sweetheart, how are you?'

She turned towards her father with a smile and leant forward to accept the brief kiss he placed on her cheek.

He looked different, more at ease, and the dark circles beneath his eyes were no longer evident. Also gone was the haunted look of previous weeks.

'This is nice,' Andre complimented as she deftly removed a fresh crusty baguette and a bottle of wine.

'I hope you're hungry.' She slid a gourmet cheesecake from the deli in the refrigerator to chill. Next she put the salad ingredients aside to rinse and added a marinade to the steak.

'Efficient, generous,' her father added. 'You didn't need to go to any trouble.'

She cast him an amused look. 'Steak and salad isn't a big deal.'

'Would you like a cup of tea? I'll make it, shall I?'

'Later,' she suggested. 'It'll be six by the time I fix dinner, then we can relax. OK with you?'

'Fine. I had an early lunch.'

Romy stored the extra groceries she'd bought in the pantry and heard his protest. 'You don't need to do that.'

'You'd deny my help, when you funded me through university and a gap year abroad?'

'My obligation as a caring parent.' His features assumed a stricken expression. 'Something you've repaid a thousand-fold.'

She met it head-on. 'By marrying Xavier to save you from a jail sentence?' she managed lightly and even managed a musing smile. 'He's wealthy, I get to live in a beautiful mansion and mix with the social elite.'

Andre made a dismissive gesture. 'None of which bears any importance to you at all.'

True, she admitted silently. Possessions, status meant little. It had always been the degree of compassion, empathy and generosity of spirit that had attracted her to people...regardless of their position in life.

'Does he treat you well?'

A loaded question, if ever there was one, and she didn't evade it. 'Yes,' she said truthfully. The resultant emotional upheaval was entirely of her own making.

'You give me your word on that?'

She met his narrowed gaze with equanimity. 'Yes.' Xavier might be a ruthless power broker in business, but demeaning or ill-treating women didn't form part of his psyche.

A change of subject was essential, and she gestured towards the adjoining dining room. 'Why don't you set the table, then open the wine to let it breathe a little?'

For a moment she thought he might persist with the personal queries, yet his hesitation proved momentary before he acceded to her suggestion.

Romy felt comfortable in the apartment, and it was pleasant to have free rein in the kitchen. She slid the baguette into the oven to warm, completed the salad preparation, then heated the skillet for the steak.

'Perhaps a glass of wine as we wait?'

Andre retrieved two goblets, part-filled them with red-bodied wine, then handed her one.

In time-honoured fashion she touched the rim of her goblet to his in a silent *salute* before savouring a sip and uttered an appreciative murmur as it slid smoothly down her throat.

'Mmm, nice.' Romy put the goblet to one side as she tended to the steak.

Nice became the operative word as they savoured the food, sipped the excellent wine, and shared companionable conversation.

Good to discover Andre seemed intent on putting his time to good use, with an early morning walk along the beach, surfing the Net, and maintaining contact with the few friends who'd elected to stand by him.

His colour had improved, and, unless she was mistaken, he'd added some weight to his lean frame.

Although she was conscious of a gap with the absence of her late mother. A woman who'd seemed more like an older sibling than a maternal figure, so close had been their bond.

Since Romy's return to Melbourne, each conversation with Andre had focused on his impending dilemma, what could possibly be done to alleviate it…and the ensuing ultimatum imposed by Xavier.

The opportunity to share time free from anxiety had been minimal, and now there was the mutual pleasure of indulging in a few *remember when* reminiscences.

The time her parents had gifted her a much-wanted puppy; the stray kitten she'd rescued and begged to keep…and the shared laughter when pup and kitten had bonded and become inseparable.

The good times: holidays, scholastic achievements. Her very first boyfriend.

'A nerd,' Romy remembered with an impish grin. 'He wore thick black-rimmed glasses and was impossibly earnest. But he was a whizz with computers and could recite facts at the drop of a hat.'

'You liked him,' Andre recalled.

'He was kind, a loyal friend.' Their first stolen kiss had been less than momentous and exceedingly awkward. Not at all what she'd hoped for, and failed even with practice to become the perfect kiss some of the girls in her class had raved about.

The gap year in France had provided a different perspective on the kissing game and had proved beyond doubt that it was a finessed sensual art not all men acquired. Given a choice, she'd preferred a gentle touch and had pushed away any male who'd attempted a deep devouring.

Until Xavier. Who'd captivated, enchanted…and held the power to melt her bones. A complete meshing of the mind and emotions, ensuring it became so much *more* than she'd believed possible.

He still did, she owned with silent reluctance…despite her every reason to hate him. All it took was a look, the lightest touch…and she was gone. *His*…like a moth drawn to flame.

Not, Romy decided, a *comfortable* reflection, given that his image worked against her and provided too vivid a reminder for her peace of mind.

There was a need for distraction, and she stood to her feet and began stacking plates and flatware, then carried them to the servery. 'Coffee? I'll set it up while I do the dishes. Go sit in the lounge, and I'll bring it in when I'm done.'

The wine had a mellowing effect which coffee failed to diminish, and the thought of sleeping alone in Xavier's large home held little appeal.

'Would you mind if I invited myself to stay over?' It was late, almost eleven, and the thought of curling up on the sofa held definite appeal.

'You need to ask? I'll get you sheets and a blanket,' Andre declared and suited words to action.

'I'll text Maria.' It was late, but at least the housekeeper would discover the message early in the morning.

All bases covered, Romy thought as she said 'goodnight' to her father, then settled comfortably in readiness to sleep.

Only to have the insistent burr of her cellphone pull her into wakefulness. *Who* would call her at this hour of night? Not Maria, she deduced as she dived into her bag and retrieved the phone, checked the displayed ID, and felt her stomach execute a somersault.

Xavier.

For one wild moment her brain went into crazy mode as a few scenarios flashed through her mind…each of them increasingly more dire as she pressed the connection.

'Hi.'

'Where are you?' His voice was a dangerous silken drawl that sent shivers scudding down her spine.

'*Hello* to you, too.'

'Romy.'

How was it possible for a single word to hold such deadly warning? She experienced a terrible need to best him. 'Out,' she managed calmly. 'Clubbing the night away with friends.'

There followed a few seconds of telling silence. 'Be grateful I'm several thousand kilometres away,' he offered with chilling softness, and she deliberately lowered her voice.

'Just as well. The temptation to *hit* you would be impossible to resist.'

'Careful, *querida.*'

'Ah.' She lowered her voice to a sultry purr. 'You miss me.'

'So brave from a distance,' he gently mocked. 'A few more days and I'll be home.'

'So soon?'

'You'll keep.'

'For your information,' she relayed quietly. 'I cooked

dinner for my father at the apartment, we shared a bottle of wine, I decided not to drive. I sent Maria a text.'

'In future, keep me in the loop.'

The silk was still evident, so too the drawl.

'Likewise,' she copied sweetly. 'Provide me with a detailed account of your whereabouts and with whom. Twenty-four seven,' she added with deliberate emphasis. 'Goodnight.'

As she cut the connection, she was willing to swear she heard his soft laughter.

Damn him. Who did he think he was?

It was a silent vent requiring no answer. And she hit her pillow, then thumped it hard. It wasn't a substitute for a vulnerable part of his anatomy…but it helped.

Romy woke early next morning, showered, dressed, replaced the blanket and pillow, and was in the midst of brewing fresh coffee when Andre entered the kitchen.

'Hi,' she greeted with a smile. 'Coffee's almost ready. Did you sleep well?'

He inclined his head and cast her a puzzled glance. 'I thought I heard a phone ring last night.'

She placed bread in the toaster. 'My cellphone.'

His eyes narrowed. 'Nothing wrong, I hope?'

'Xavier,' she enlightened him wryly and saw his frown. 'You hadn't told him you were here?'

'He's in New York,' she reminded him as the toast popped, and she added a nutritious spread, then bit into it.

Andre looked at her carefully. 'Whatever you're planning…don't.'

Her gaze was remarkably level. 'I don't see the need to relay my every move.'

'Tread carefully,' he warned gently. 'Xavier can be a very dangerous man when crossed.'

'Cereal and juice?' she queried. It wasn't an avoidance tactic, she assured herself silently, merely a diversion. 'Or would you like bacon and eggs?'

'Cereal. I'll get it. What time do you need to leave?'

'Soon.' She took another bite of toast, then she poured coffee into two cups and handed him one. 'I'll call in, check with Maria, and change into fresh clothes.'

It was seven when she left the apartment, and three quarters of an hour later she was on the road again.

As days went, the following few were pretty run-of-the-mill, in that she taught school, marked homework, ate dinner on her own, researched on the Net, checked the next day's lessons, then retired to bed.

Romy had thought she'd relish Xavier's absence, and while the days didn't bother her...the nights did.

She hated to admit it, but the bed seemed overly large without him in it. She missed his body warmth, the way his arms curved her close in the night. The brush of his lips, the sweep of his hands as they traced her body.

His possession.

Dear heaven. Just thinking about him made her hunger for his touch...for each day she became more emotionally restless with need.

It was crazy, but she resorted to exchanging bed-pillows so she rested her head on the one he used, almost as if the faint lingering smell of his soap might soothe her senses and aid an easy sleep.

His calls were infrequent, their exchanged text and e-mail messages brief, and Kassi's invitation to join her at a gallery exhibition was received with enthusiasm.

Formal dress, Kassi advised, and Romy selected a classic black dress, applied light make-up with emphasis on her eyes, twisted her hair into a careless knot and fixed it with a large clip, added minimal jewellery, stepped into stilettos and caught up a black evening purse.

She turned…and came to an abrupt halt at the sight of Xavier standing with one shoulder propped against the door frame as he regarded her with indolent ease.

For one heart-stopping second she felt like a startled rabbit caught frozen in the headlights of a car.

'Going somewhere?'

To utter 'you're home' seemed superfluous. 'Kassi has tickets to a gallery exhibition.'

He moved away from the door frame and discarded his jacket. 'I'm sure she won't mind if I join you.' The tie was pulled free and cast aside. 'Call her.'

His tone was even, calm…but there was a predatory edge apparent that made her incredibly wary.

'You've just come off a long international flight.'

One eyebrow arched in silent mockery. 'During which I slept for a few hours.' He tossed his shirt and toed off his shoes. 'I'll hit the shower, then dress.' He freed the zip fastening and stepped out of his trousers. 'Fifteen minutes.'

He was ready in less, looking incredible in a black tailored evening suit and crisp white linen, and she watched as he pocketed a billfold, then caught up his keys.

'Let's go. Where, precisely?'

She relayed the name and address of the gallery, and sat in silence as the Mercedes purred through the city streets.

Anything she thought of by way of conversation seemed banal, yet her nerves screamed with the need to cut the tension.

'You could have told me you'd be home this evening.'

'I didn't consider it necessary.'

'Of course not. You expected a dutiful wife quietly marking school papers while she pined for your return.'

The tone was sweet, but it held a sting, and she incurred his dark glance.

'Dutiful and pine are not two descriptions I'd choose for you.'

'Sassy, prickly?'

'Apt.'

The gallery was situated in a trendy inner-city suburb, and Xavier slid the car into a parking space.

There were several guests present as she entered the tastefully furnished gallery. City scions and patrons of the arts mingling as they offered sage opinions of the work on display.

'Romy. Xavier.'

Kassi's bubbly voice acted like a breath of fresh air, and Romy turned to receive an enthusiastic greeting, then watched as Xavier brushed his lips to Kassi's cheek.

'You probably know most of the guests,' Kassi continued warmly as a waiter appeared and proffered a drinks tray. 'Champagne to lighten the mood, or,' she paused and lowered her voice with an impish grin, 'enhance the need to express due praise for even the most hideous item.'

'Hush your mouth,' Romy reproved, making a *volteface*. 'You did say a percentage of the ticket price aids a worthwhile charity.'

'Plus fifteen percent of every item sold.'

'Well, there you go.' Romy managed a brilliant smile.

'Worthy is good.'

'Hideous could well prove to be a good conversation piece,' Xavier drawled as he declined champagne in favour of orange juice.

Kassi laughed. 'Surely you jest?'

'Not entirely.' He indicated the paintings displayed along one wall. 'Shall we?'

A photographer snapped away at the beautiful people,

who, with practiced smiles and the *right* pose, would feature in the media social pages.

Including, it appeared, Xavier DeVasquez and his wife.

Romy summoned a stunning smile and managed to hold it in place as Xavier curved an arm at her waist and drew her close.

The visual attestation of a happily married couple?

Perhaps, she conceded, although *happy* was a fallacy.

Would it ever be any different?

'I've already scoped out some of the sculptures,' Kassi began as an acquaintance engaged Xavier in conversation. 'Come have a look. One is quite stunning.'

Stone, and beautifully curved, it was a work of art, although they each gave a rueful smile at the price.

'Xavier arrived home unexpectedly,' Kassi noted. 'Exuding enough sexual energy to be flattering.'

Romy executed an effective eye roll. 'You think?'

'Sweetheart, don't you *see* the way he looks at you?'

'I imagine he can't wait to get me home so he can wring my neck for not keeping him in the loop,' she replied and wrinkled her nose at the faint gleam apparent in Kassi's eyes.

'And what loop would that be?'

'Updating him on my social activities.'

'Ah.'

'Which is supposed to mean?'

'He cares?' Kassi deliberately waited a beat. 'It's not your neck he wants to wring?'

'Sure. And pigs fly.'

'They do, too,' Kassi argued impishly. 'In animated cartoons.'

'Hah.'

Xavier joined them seconds later. 'Interesting conversation?'

'Four-legged flying animals,' Kassi said with a perfectly straight face.

The corners of his mouth tilted with humour. 'Perhaps coffee might be a wiser option than more champagne.'

'Coffee would be good.'

It was after eleven when they took their leave and accompanied Kassi to her car, and the girls hugged and promised to be in touch *soon*. Romy merely smiled at Kassi's 'take care of *you'* and kept the smile in place as Kassi ignited the engine.

'Home,' Xavier announced succinctly as they walked to where the Mercedes was parked.

'Why don't you get it over with?' Romy confronted him as he eased the car onto the street.

'What, in particular, are you referring to?'

'You've been *simmering* all evening.'

'You imagine I object to you attending tonight's function with Kassi?'

'Naturally you return to your hotel room alone.'

'Are you accusing me of infidelity?'

'Like I'd ever know?'

He bit back a vicious oath. 'Marriage involves trust.'

'But we don't have a normal marriage.'

He speared her a dark glance. 'Since when did you gain that impression?'

'How is it normal?' It was a cry from the heart, born of tension, and she stared out the windscreen in silence as he covered the distance to Brighton at the designated speed limit, used the remote to open the gates to his residence, and drew the car to a halt inside the garage. Romy entered the foyer in silence, only to gasp in outraged surprise as he simply lifted and positioned her over one shoulder, then ascended the staircase.

'What do you think you're doing?' She punched a fist against his ribs. 'Put me down!'

'Soon.'

'Xavier!' Kicking her way to the bedroom wasn't exactly on her agenda, nor were strong-arm tactics. 'You *macho* fiend!'

He reached the top of the stairs and turned towards the main bedroom.

'Are you *done?*'

'With you?' He slid her down to stand on her feet before him. '*Amante,* I haven't even begun.'

His head descended and he took her mouth in a kiss that rocked her very being. Deep, so impossibly deep…possessive in a manner that stamped his ownership and plundered with a hungry urgency meant to conquer. And did.

Hungry, frankly sensual and infinitely primal.

When at last he lifted his head, she almost drowned in the smouldering intensity evident in his dark eyes, and she uttered a protesting gasp as he lowered his head and closed his mouth over her own in a soothing touch that caressed and teased with unhurried warmth.

His hands framed her face. 'Better. But not nearly enough. Clothes, *querida.* Yours. Mine. Now.'

It was difficult to know who removed what, only that soon every last vestige of clothing lay scattered on the carpet.

'All week,' he said huskily, 'each night…*this* is what has kept me sane. *You.* Beneath me, in command, taking the ride of your life. Anywhere, as long as it meant I was inside you.'

He drew her down onto the bed with him and indulged in a sensual tasting of all her most intimate pleasure pulses, bringing her to fever pitch again and again until she begged for his possession in guttural cries she failed to recognize as her own.

Only then did he enter her, easing in until she took all of him, and the first orgasm came swiftly, taking her high on an emotional tide that slowly ebbed before he built it again in long, strong strokes until she became mindless. *His,* as he took his own pleasure and enhanced her own with an electrifying passion that left them both incandescent and gasping for breath.

Even then he wasn't content, and she almost sobbed as he trailed light kisses to each breast, savoured the sensitive peaks, then moved low to gift the most intimate kiss of all. Using his tongue, the edge of his teeth until she shattered.

Afterwards, he wrapped his arms about her slim form and held her as they subsided into the sleep of the exhausted.

CHAPTER TEN

A MID-WEEK invitation to dinner ensured Romy took care with her make-up, keeping it subtle with emphasis on her eyes, a touch of bronze at her cheeks and a light gloss on her lips.

Upswept hair and stilettos added essential height to her petite shape, and the ice-blue gown with its delicate spray of minute crystals looked suitably elegant to wear to a private dinner held in their hosts' home.

A touch of delicate perfume, and she was ready to go.

'Beautiful,' Xavier complimented her, and she turned towards him with a faint smile.

'Thank you.'

The black dinner suit bore an expensive cut and was undoubtedly tailor-made to fit as superbly as it did, enhancing his breadth of shoulder and the inherent strength of his powerful frame. Stark white linen provided a contrast to his olive skin and broad-boned facial features.

The expensive trappings of a sophisticated man, Romy mused...aware nothing could tame the magnetic quality apparent in those dark, gleaming eyes. Or dim the overwhelming sexuality he projected with no visible effort.

'Shall we leave?'

Their hosts resided in Toorak, a well-established suburb

with tree-lined streets and beautiful homes. Money, old money…the elite kind, considered a snobbish cut above those who numbered among the *nouveau riche*.

Romy was capable of holding her own in any social situation. Yet for some reason the nerves in her stomach were having a field day as Xavier drew the Mercedes to a smooth halt in the curved driveway of a magnificent double-storied sandstone mansion.

Elegance personified, she perceived as they were greeted by a uniformed butler and welcomed into the spacious marble-tiled foyer. A double, curving staircase, a chandelier, original works of old masters and imported French furniture.

'The guests are gathered in the lounge,' the butler informed them. 'If you'll follow me?'

It was a large room. Imposing, Romy added to herself, as he opened the French doors.

'Ma'am, sir. Romy and Xavier DeVasquez.'

A beautifully attired woman glided forward, accompanied by an older man whose welcoming smile seemed genuine.

'Xavier. So pleased you could join us. And this is Romy, your lovely wife.' He extended his hand, which Romy accepted.

'Gerard. Stephanie,' Xavier acknowledged smoothly.

Gerard indicated the assembled guests. 'You know everyone here. Do make yourselves comfortable.'

Was it her imagination, or did Xavier's presence arouse interest from all of the women present? Not that she could blame them…he was something else, and his New York roots merely added a certain intrigue.

Seven for seven-thirty allowed time to mix and mingle whilst sipping vintage wine and indulging in conversation.

The last guest and her partner made something of a

grand entrance…on the verge of being late, but nonetheless apologetic.

Model, actress…or both, Romy perceived, for the tall, svelte young woman displayed a gorgeous figure in a designer gown that shaped her curves and clung to an impressive cleavage that seemed a little *too* perfect.

Auburn hair tumbled in waves down her back, and her make-up appeared flawless.

The man at her side was picture-book handsome, a little too smooth, too practiced, and, unless she was mistaken, there merely as a foil.

'I'm *so* sorry we're late.' Her voice was a sultry purr, her smile dazzling. 'We were caught in traffic.'

No, Romy silently amended…you intended to make an *entrance.* And succeeded beyond measure…except there was no camera evident to record it.

Lose the cynicism, Romy chastised. It was not an admirable trait!

Chanel, for that was her name, became the focus of the evening, and she played her part to perfection. A part calculated to galvanize the attention of every man present.

Her target, for women of Chanel's calibre usually had one, was Xavier. Or was it only Romy who noticed the subtle glances, the thinly disguised avaricious by-play employed to gain his attention?

The fact Chanel's companion, Alex, appeared a little too fascinated with a need to observe Romy's reaction suggested their combined act formed part of a deliberate game…and not a very pleasant one.

If *entertainment* was the subtle focus, then Romy would play…by her own rules.

Seating at the dining table placed Chanel and Alex directly opposite, Romy and Xavier, an arrangement Chanel engineered, dismissing name-card placements with an elegant gesture of her hand.

'Darling, placement cards are so…incredibly formal, don't you think?'

Stephanie, who doubtless had put much effort into the seating gave a graceful lift of one eyebrow. 'I prefer to ensure the comfort of my guests.'

A subtle sting, but one nonetheless.

It was, however, Chanel's show, something which became apparent as the dinner progressed. A very leisurely meal, given there were numerous courses…impeccably presented food prepared, presumably, by a master chef and served by uniformed waitstaff.

'Tell us, sweetie,' Chanel said to Romy with a cajoling purr, 'how you managed to drag the gorgeous Xavier to the altar.'

Verbal swords at dusk? 'Would you believe I was the reluctant one, and it was Xavier who did the dragging?' Romy parried with deliberate sweetness.

The lift of an expressive eyebrow conveyed disbelief. 'How—out of character.'

'You think?'

'What a shame I spent a month soaking up the sun in Barbados.'

Or you could have provided competition? 'Ah, but Barbados is so tempting. And life is filled with lost opportunities, don't you agree?'

Alex cast her a lazily appreciative smile, which Romy chose to ignore…instinctively aware that only a fool took an eye from the figurative ball when Chanel chose to *play*.

'I seem to recall your—er—relationship with Xavier failed to bring commitment first time round.' Chanel paused for effect, her smile overly bright. 'Are you going to share your secret?'

Romy appeared to give the request consideration before declaring an overly polite—'No.'

Chanel took a few seconds to examine her lacquered nails. '*Interesting* how your father's…indiscretion, shall we say,' she paused momentarily, 'no longer has a court date. Whatever ploy you devised, darling. It obviously worked.'

'Would you care to be specific?' Romy queried sweetly.

'Conjecture makes for fascinating conversation, don't you think?'

'If the objective is to denigrate.' She deliberately allowed her gaze to rove from guest to guest until she reached full circle. 'If anyone has further questions, I suggest you raise them now.' There was a deathly silence. 'No?' She managed a credible smile. 'Then perhaps we can declare the subject closed.'

Alex began to clap to a slow beat before offering, with thinly veiled mockery. 'Well fielded, Romy.'

In what capacity had he accompanied Chanel? As a friend, lover? Arm candy…or merely a social handbag?

'Catching balls is one of my acquired skills.' There, make of that what you will!

The number of courses seemed interminable, and it took an effort to consume a portion from each one as she was drawn into conversation. Questions about schools, the art of teaching, and she shared a few anecdotes that drew several smiles and some laughter.

'Your wife is quite the raconteur,' one of the male guests offered by way of a compliment, which drew agreement, and it was something of a relief when the meal came to a conclusion and the guests were invited to adjourn to the lounge for coffee.

It was almost midnight when Xavier indicated the need to leave, and Romy thanked their hosts, acknowledged the remaining guests, and accompanied Xavier to their car.

She chose silence during the drive home, aware that if she resorted to speech she'd probably utter something regrettable.

'No comment, *pequeña?*' Xavier posed as he drew the Mercedes to a halt in the garage.

'On the trial by fire?' She sent him a dark glance that had no effect whatsoever. 'You could have supported me.'

'You were coping admirably on your own.'

Thanks for nothing. 'The woman is a bitch!'

'Chanel?'

'Who else? She obviously felt she had a claim.' She wouldn't ask, told herself she didn't care…and knew she lied.

'Only in her mind.'

'Why do I find that difficult to believe.' It was a statement, not a query, and his mouth curved a little as he captured her chin between thumb and forefinger, tilting it so she met his dark gaze.

'I choose not to go where countless men have been before.'

Oh, my.

'Does that answer your question?'

One of them.

Romy released her seatbelt, undid the door clasp and slid to her feet, aware Xavier copied her actions.

The foyer was lit, awaiting their arrival, and she moved towards the staircase as he reset the alarm.

The large bed looked inviting, and she shed the stilettos, followed them with her clothes and made for the *en suite* where she removed her make-up and reached for the pins in her hair.

Only to find Xavier there, his fingers dispensing with her own as he completed the task.

He'd discarded his clothes, with the exception of black briefs, and she met his darkening gaze.

'If this is foreplay, you're wasting your time,' she managed in a stiff voice as he shaped her shoulders.

'Why, when it gives us both pleasure?'

He lowered his head and touched his lips to the vulnerable curve at the edge of her neck.

At the same time he cupped each breast and teased the sensitive peaks and felt them tighten. Sensed her faint indrawn breath…and trailed his mouth to the sensitive place behind one ear.

With infinite care he slid one hand down to her waist, lingered there, then slipped slowly to rest at the blonde curls at the apex of her thighs.

His hand lowered a little as he slid one finger between the sensitive folds and felt the instinctive tightening of highly sensitized muscles.

'Want me to stop?' He eased two fingers deep inside, heard her faint gasp, and began a rhythmic stimulation designed to drive her wild.

'No…damn you.' The breath hissed through her teeth as he deftly turned her to face him.

He took her mouth with his own in an erotic kiss as he brought her to climax. Then he captured her waist, positioned her carefully to accept his turgid length…and surged in to the hilt.

She shook her head, and her hair swung from side to side as he began to move, and it was he who drew in a deep breath as she sank her teeth into him.

'You want to play?'

It was crazy to traverse that path. For it led to a long, leisurely and highly erotic tasting designed to drive her to the edge of emotional sanity.

Yet some devilish imp compelled her…and this time it was she who bucked against him as he sought the sensitive swell of her breast, nibbled a little, then nipped with the edge of his teeth before shifting to take the hardened peak into his mouth and shamelessly sucking until she whimpered for him to stop.

Without a word he carried her into the bedroom and tumbled them both down onto the bed.

It became more than she needed…much more, and it was she who begged for his possession as he brought her body so incredibly *alive;* she became aware of every sensitive nerve and pulse, each distinct beat of her heart. Dear heaven, every skin cell. *His,* solely his.

Afterwards he curved her close against him, drew up the bedcovers, and extinguished the lights, then he trailed a hand slowly down her back until her breathing eased and she fell asleep.

He should check the overseas markets, make a few calls, shift some funds and transfer stock. Except it could wait.

The comfort and well-being of the woman in his arms held more importance.

So petite, he mused as he touched his lips to her forehead. Slender, with delicate curves. Generous and giving, with an inner strength he had long admired.

She touched him in places no other woman ever had. Creeping beneath his skin, invading his senses and threatening his very existence. He, who had never relied on anyone since the very early days of his life. Having learnt the hard way the only one he could trust was himself. A defence mechanism that prevented him from allowing anyone to come too close.

It had earned him the ruthless tag in the business arena…and while his bedroom techniques were lauded by the women he'd bedded, those who dared accused him of missing a sensitivity chip.

Affection, fondness…he could feel those emotions.

He'd been Romy's first lover. A rare gift, especially from a young woman in her twenties. He'd experienced a need to protect and care for her…and he had, until she'd walked.

Because he hadn't been able to give her what she'd wanted.

Not marriage…or even commitment.

Just his love.

Romy's last class for the day was Grade twelve English. A class where a few students chose to give her a hard time. It wasn't personal…any teacher who taught this particular group incurred lack of interest, heckling and general misbehaviour.

Ten minutes in, and she needed to marshal all her resources to provide a degree of order. After another ten minutes, she was strongly tempted to cut to the chase and turn the five miscreants in to the principal.

Instead, she challenged them to take one of Shakespeare's sonnets and change the words to gangsta rap idiom. It had worked with a previous class. Possibly it might hit the mark with this one.

'Gettin' with it, teach?'

'It's language, bud,' she responded without missing a beat. 'Show me what you can do.'

'Don't know if I want to.'

'No prob. Just do the curriculum version.'

He eyeballed her, weighed up his options, then he took up paper and pen, opened the textbook, chose the specified page, rolled his eyes…and appeared to check the first line.

Not so Ace, the known leader of the five, a gangly youth

with attitude who'd learnt to cover his dyslexia well. There was help available, and she'd approached him about it, offered to consult with his parents, only to have him resort to denial and belligerence. The fact she *knew* of his dyslexia worked as a mark against her, and his defence mechanism ensured he made her life during class as difficult as possible.

Today was no exception, and the fact that one of his gang of five had defected, so to speak, at her suggestion, only made it worse, and he began tapping his desk in a rhythmic beat, increasing the volume until it reached a crescendo.

'You might want to stop that.' Romy's voice held a tone that promised action, and he merely smirked.

'Whatcha goin' to do, teach? Suspend me?'

'Why would I do what you want?'

'Cos then I get to hang…way out of this hellhole.'

She deliberately arched an eyebrow. 'On a one-way ticket to police detention…next step jail?'

'Roof over my head, three square, and a prison tatt.'

Not to mention the hardened criminals who'd regard him as fresh meat.

'You want a lecture?' One she was compelled to give. Except reverse psychology occasionally hit the mark when little else did. 'You make your own choices, Ace,' she said quietly in the hope it would sink in.

At least he didn't lurch to his feet and stomp out.

Instead he saved the anger for when the buzzer announced the end of the school day, and as the students filed out, he ensured he was last, shifting close to where she stood.

For a moment he just subjected her to a hard look, then he deliberately shouldered her to the floor…and added insult to injury by laughing as he went through the door.

Hell.

Romy picked herself up, smoothed a hand over her clothes, winced a little as she slid paperwork into her satchel, and ran a quick eye over the empty desks before heading for a scheduled teachers' meeting.

One which ran over time and ensured she encountered peak-hour traffic during the drive home.

Since when had she begun thinking of Xavier's Brighton mansion as *home?* she reflected as her Mini Cooper languished among many vehicles forming a long line at a traffic intersection. An unconscious acknowledgement she'd accepted his terms…when she wasn't sure she *had?*

If only…except she didn't do *if only* any more. Life was *now,* the day, and whatever transpired, for survival of self meant dealing with the bad and focusing on the good stuff.

Psychology 101, she perceived as the line of traffic in front of her began to move.

It was almost six when she entered the foyer, and she made for the kitchen and checked in with Maria, then she ran lightly upstairs to the master suite.

A leisurely hot shower would do wonders, and she discarded her clothes, set the water dial to *hot,* and stepped beneath its flow.

Romy lathered shampoo into her hair, and soon the rose-scented soap she favoured filled the room.

It felt good, and she stretched to iron out the kinks, inordinately glad the day was almost over. Soon she'd enjoy a pleasant meal, after which she'd retreat to mark homework, then maybe slot a DVD into the player and relax.

Pleasant thoughts, she perceived as she used a towel to remove the moisture from her body, then she secured it sarong-fashion, blow-dried her hair, and emerged into the bedroom to find Xavier in the process of discarding his clothes.

He regarded her with a warmth that set her pulse moving up a notch.

'Pity,' he drawled. 'I was about to join you.'

'Sex in the shower…before dinner?'

His husky laugh almost undid her. 'You disapprove?'

That was the thing, she thought silently. She exulted in his touch, adored what they shared…even though it was becoming increasingly difficult to distance the desires of her body from the dictates of her head.

There was a danger in thinking too much. Analyzing each word, his every action, for it served little purpose.

Men, she perceived, were driven by sexual pleasure… while women required emotional involvement.

Romy offered him a winsome smile. 'I'd prefer to eat, sip a glass of wine…' She trailed to a halt and regarded him pensively. 'Perhaps when I'm done marking homework, I'll consider the sex thing.'

Xavier closed the distance between them and cradled her face between his hands. 'Consider, hmm?' His mouth closed over hers, briefly, teasing in a manner that made her want more.

Then he released her and walked naked into the *en suite*. Seconds later she heard the shower, and his powerful image came too readily to mind as she shed the towel and dressed in jeans and a fashionable top.

She slid her feet into comfortable flats, added a touch of gloss to her lips, then she ran lightly downstairs to help Maria with the table.

Xavier entered the dining room as Romy placed a serving dish containing an aromatic paella on the table, and he tended to the wine.

It was a pleasant meal, the paella a delight to the palate, and the wine helped soothe the cares of the day.

Afterwards they took coffee, and Xavier retreated to his home office while Romy returned upstairs to mark home-work assignments.

It took a while, longer than she'd anticipated, and when she came to a page with a profanity written in bold letters, she simply scrunched it into a ball and binned it.

Ace. It had to be. It fit—an expressive action deliber-ately designed to goad her.

Except it hadn't worked. He wanted a reaction, and ignoring the missive would be more effective than any chastising punishment she could offer.

It was late when she heard Xavier enter the room, and she glanced up as he crossed to her side.

'How long before you're through?'

Romy checked her list. 'Two to go, then I'm done.'

He placed a hand on her shoulder, and she couldn't prevent a faint gasp of pain.

'You've hurt yourself?'

She attempted a light shrug as he tilted her face towards him. 'I knocked it against something.'

'Knocked it against what?' he demanded quietly, and his eyes narrowed a little. 'Where? At school? During class?'

'Will you stop with the twenty questions?' she pro-tested. 'I fell. It's just a bruise.'

He released her, and she returned her attention to the as-signment, read and marked it, and added it to the others.

Last one, thank heavens, as she looked at the paper…only for the breath to hitch in her throat at the sight of yet another note.

The words were neatly printed, as the previous notes had been, the message similar.

'Is this the first?'

He had the silent tread of a cat…a very large jungle cat, she perceived as he towered over her.

'Romy?'

She could tell he wasn't going to let it go, and she turned to face him. 'I've had a few. Like this,' she indicated the note. 'Slipped in among homework.'

'You've kept them?'

She inclined her head. 'They're in my satchel.'

'Show me.'

She retrieved them and handed them to him, watching as he read each one.

'You don't know who wrote them?'

She met his level gaze. 'It could be anyone.'

'Do you have any suspicion as to who it might be?'

Ace? It wasn't his writing. But that didn't exclude him. 'No.'

'Have you reported it?'

'Not yet.'

His expression hardened. 'Do it, Romy. Or I will.'

'My territory, my problem.'

'So butt out?'

'*Yes.*'

'On the condition you tell me if any more notes appear.'

'Yessir.'

He curved a hand to her cheek and pressed his thumb against the centre of her lower lip. 'When you're done, I'll check your shoulder.'

He was too much…too close. And the temptation to nip his thumb with the edge of her teeth was irresistible.

His eyes darkened, and for a moment she thought he meant to seek retribution. Except he merely crossed the room and began shedding his clothes…an action which tore her concentration level to shreds.

She managed to mark the final paper, then collected her papers and stowed them in her satchel. Then *she* emerged from the bathroom minutes later, attired in a sleep singlet and light cotton sleep trousers.

It was impossible to avoid Xavier's attention as he probed the slight swelling surrounding her shoulder. The bruise would be a doozy, and she deliberately avoided meeting his gaze.

'Whatever you're not telling me,' he said with silky indolence. 'I suggest you do…soon.'

'Or else you'll play the heavy?'

'With you? No.'

For a moment she couldn't think of a single word.

The air between them became electric, and she stood locked in its thrall, unable to move. He managed to attack the fragile tenure of her control, his disruptive sensuality a potent force that captured her emotions and made her incapable of rational thought.

There was only him and a capricious consuming need.

'Come to bed,' he said gently. 'It's late, and we both need to sleep.'

Sleep? He could arouse her with a *look* that promised much…then calmly suggest they *sleep?*

He had to be joking!

Except he merely drew her close when they slid beneath the bedcovers, doused the light, pressed his lips to her forehead…and within minutes his breathing steadied, his heartbeat slowed, and he slept.

How did he do that?

CHAPTER ELEVEN

FORMAL, on this occasion, meant dressing up, Romy conceded, aware she'd almost reached the end of her evening wear selection as she selected a red gown in silk chiffon with a ruched bodice held by spaghetti straps and a skirt that fell from the waist in layers to her feet. Her only jewellery was a small diamond pendant on a delicate gold chain with matching ear-studs gifted by her parents for her twenty-first birthday.

The auction fundraiser drew invitation-only attendance by the city's social elite, given the number of guests milling outside the hotel's function room.

The nominated charity for tonight's event was in aid of children stricken with leukaemia, while the auction itself featured a selection of donated antique furniture and valuable *objets d'art*.

Items, catalogued and priced according to valuation, were displayed in colour within a glossy folder gifted to each guest on entry.

Waiters circled the lounge offering trays filled with flutes of champagne and orange juice, while waitresses bore platters containing a variety of canapés to sample.

An hour was designated for personal inspection of the

items on display, cleverly allocated to allow guests to peruse the folder beforehand.

Efficient planning was key, Romy noted as she wandered past the items at Xavier's side.

'Do you see anything you like?'

A small, beautifully crafted *escritoire* featuring delicate inlays in contrasting wood, token drawers, and slender carved legs.

The valuation figure was expensive. Too expensive for her to fund from her teacher's salary, and she refused to ask Xavier to gift it to her.

'Alex, come have a look at this.'

Chanel? The sultry purr was one of a kind, and Romy felt her heart sink as the pair joined them.

Air kisses were exchanged, and Chanel's immaculately lacquered fingers drifted down Xavier's arm and lingered a little too long.

'What a coincidence to see you both here,' Alex drawled, although Romy doubted coincidence had much to do with it, despite Chanel and Alex forming part of the A-list guests.

'Isn't it exquisite?' Chanel observed, indicating the *escritoire*. 'I want it.'

Chanel, it soon became clear, had a purpose…to test her flirting skills on Xavier.

To give him credit, he didn't respond. A short while later she rested a hand on the lapel of his jacket and made a play of tracing the seam. A hand he deliberately removed.

Ten minutes in, and Romy decided she didn't have to remain by his side and watch the game Chanel had chosen to play out in public.

'If you'll excuse me,' Romy offered sweetly. 'I'll go check out the items.'

She bore Xavier's studied look with equanimity and bade Chanel a light, 'Have fun.' A mixed message, if ever there was one. Did the model imagine Romy was blind, for heaven's sake?

'I'll join you,' Xavier said smoothly and curved an arm along the back of her waist. 'If you'll excuse us?'

An act of proprietorial togetherness?

As if Chanel would take the hint!

She didn't. 'Let's browse together.' She spared Romy a taunting glance. 'So much more fun.'

Romy barely controlled the itch to give her a stinging slap…but in company it really wasn't a polite thing to do. Instead, she merely offered a smile and pretended for the ensuing half hour to show an interest in every item.

Consequently it came as a relief when it was announced the auction would begin.

Items came and went, and for the most part the bidding escalated above valuation, providing a pleasing result for the charity.

The *escritoire* was the second to last item in the catalogue, and the opening bid was high. There were a number of bids, but it soon came down to Xavier and Chanel.

The figure rose to the ridiculous, more than twice the valuation…a fact which drew the attention of the guests, with whispered speculation as to who would win.

There reached a point where Chanel began to waiver, although she continued, managing to push the bid further before conceding defeat.

'That was…unwarranted,' Romy said quietly when the auctioneer declared the item sold.

'Consider it a gift,' Xavier declared with indolent ease.

She regarded him in silence for several seconds. 'It'll make a beautiful addition to your home.'

'Our home,' he corrected silkily. 'And the *escritoire* is yours.'

The money he paid went to charity, and that helped salve her conscience. 'Thank you.' Although she was far from done with him.

The fact he knew merely intensified her need to upbraid him, and she waited until he eased the Maybach away from the hotel and entered the stream of traffic vacating the inner city.

'You had no need to play Chanel at her own game.'

'No? The *escritoire* became yours from the moment you saw it.'

'And you figured that out…how?'

'You possess a very expressive face.'

She lapsed into silence and didn't break it until they ascended the staircase and reached their bedroom.

'It's an exquisite piece of furniture. Thank you for gifting it to me.'

Xavier shrugged out of his jacket, removed his tie and began loosening the buttons on his shirt as he crossed to her side.

Without a word he moved behind her and tended to the zip fastening on her gown.

'Was that so difficult?'

She didn't pretend to misunderstand. 'Thanking you? Yes.'

He slid the straps from her shoulders and the gown slithered down into a silken heap at her feet. 'Get used to it.'

Her eyes speared his. 'I have my own money.'

His hands curved over her shoulders as he impelled her close. 'You talk too much,' he said gently and laid his mouth over her own.

She lifted a fist and connected with his shoulder in silent protest. An ineffectual act she didn't repeat as one hand cupped her bottom, while the other captured her nape…and she became lost.

Caught up in the passion he was able to arouse until her body *sang* beneath his touch. Until mere *touch* wasn't enough, and her fingers reached for his remaining clothes in feverish need.

It became a feast of the senses…possessive, greedy. Then wild and wanton as he took her high, so high she had to hold on as it became too much…way too much. More than he'd ever gifted her, and she cried, unaware of the tears coursing down her cheeks until he gently brushed them with his mouth.

Afterwards she slept for a while, then drifted awake at the touch of his lips teasing the delicate hollow at the base of her throat.

This time it was she who gifted him, with an oral tasting that tested his control…and broke it, as he hauled her close and took her on the ride of her life.

Romy stirred into wakefulness at Xavier's feather-light touch, murmured something indistinct and buried her head beneath the pillow.

'Coffee, *querida*. Hot, sweet and strong.'

She groaned as he removed the pillow and plumped it against the headboard. 'It's early,' she protested and heard his husky chuckle.

'It's ten, and time to rise, shine…and go for breakfast.'

Food? He was talking food? 'Go for…?' She lifted her head and looked at him…saw that he'd showered, shaved, dressed, and looked far too indecently *alive* after a late night out.

'It's Maria's day off,' he said patiently.

Of course. Sunday. 'Are you open to negotiation?'

'Are you propositioning me?'

After last night? He had to be joking!

'I take it that's a *no?*' His smile held warmth and a degree of lingering passion as he removed the bedcovers.

'Hey!'

A hand curved over her bottom, squeezed gently, and made her yelp in protest.

'Here's the day's plan,' Xavier drawled with a degree of humour. 'We have brunch at one of Brighton's superb cafés, take in a set of tennis this afternoon, after which I'll cook steaks on the barbecue while you toss a salad.'

'Not sure about the tennis.'

'You'll warm to it. Sit,' he commanded, and she obediently slid up into a sitting position, accepted the coffee and took an appreciative sip.

The caffeine hit her stomach, and by the time she'd drained the cup she felt awake, aware, and ready to face the day. 'You mentioned food?'

She hit the shower, chose casual white jeans, pulled on a knit top, slid her feet into heels, added moisturizer, a touch of lipgloss, then she caught her hair into a thick plait, collected her bag and joined Xavier in the foyer.

'We could take the Mini Cooper.'

A suggestion which incurred a wry look, and she wrinkled her nose at him. 'Just a thought.'

'Perish it.'

She offered him an impish grin as she imagined him folding his length into the passenger seat. It was a girl's car...sassy, zippy and cool. Very cool.

'Okay, so it's the Maybach.' Expensive class. *Very* expensive class.

To complement the man he'd become, she added silently. Yet to be fair, he didn't flaunt his wealth. There was no excessive jewellery, just a slim Rolex watch and his wedding ring.

He lived in a beautiful mansion, yet the interior decorating was neither overt nor overdone. His fleet of vehicles numbered one in each foreign city he owned real estate, and the Brighton garage housed only the Maybach and a four-wheel drive which Maria used to shop for groceries and anything needed in the house. The Learjet he owned was leased out to high-fliers who paid for the privilege, and, apart from international flights, he preferred to travel business class on a commercial airline.

There were worthy charities he generously supported, and he worked hard. Even now, when he could easily sit back and delegate, he chose to keep a close watch on every aspect of his vast business interests.

The sun rode high in the sky as they strolled along a trendy avenue where a number of boutique cafés sported outdoor tables beneath protective shade-umbrellas where numerous patrons sipped coffee and lingered over a meal.

Xavier indicated an empty table, ordered a full breakfast for each of them, and when it was served, they ate with enjoyment.

Melbourne weather was known to be contrary, but today the skies were almost cloudless and it was warm and sunny.

It was pleasant not to have to think of work…to view the remainder of the day with leisurely anticipation. No particular schedule, merely a loose plan, and the ability to change it as the whim took them.

'Feel better?'

Romy spared Xavier a musing look. 'Much.'

They lingered over coffee, then chose to browse the nearby shops, most of which were open to trade, and it was fun to check out some of the wares. Already there were a few Christmas items displayed, and she experienced a wistful few moments, picturing a Christmas tree festooned with tinsel and decorations…set, perhaps, in the foyer with fairy lights to illuminate its splendour at night.

It was mid-afternoon when Xavier garaged the car, and they each changed into suitable tennis gear and entered the enclosed court where, in a set Xavier was guaranteed to win, Romy managed to score a few points. He could easily have powered her off the court…instead he chose to play a tactical game, fair, yet fun, and they both emerged to don swimwear and cool off in the pool.

It was after six when, attired in casual clothes, Xavier set up the barbecue while she set a fresh, crusty baguette in the oven and began creating a delectable salad.

They ate alfresco on the terrace with its view out over Brighton beach, watching the sun go down and the tracery of street lights provide illumination along the foreshore.

There was an intimacy apparent, a close attuning of the minds that encouraged a desire for her to have him confide something of his background. His rise and rise in the business sector was well documented, but it was the early years which held her fascination.

There were almost no facts available, only that his mother had died young and there were no siblings. His decision to reside in Australia had been motivated by chance and opportunity, and he'd made it his base by choice.

Romy asked the question she'd posed a few years before…one he'd dismissed then as being a 'no-go' zone with a wryly cynical 'I am who I've become.'

'You have a burning need for me to fill in the blanks?'

'It's a part of who you are,' she opined simply.

'Poverty,' he revealed quietly. 'A trailer park existence with no father I recall, and a mother who was forced to work sixteen-hour days in order for us to survive. She died before my ninth birthday, and Children's Services farmed me out to a number of foster homes whose registered carers, in the main, valued the money they received more than a child's welfare. At fourteen I chose the streets, living by my wits and graft.' He spared her a hard look that spoke volumes. 'It wasn't a time of which I'm particularly proud.'

Romy didn't pursue the reason *why.* The scars on his body revealed enough for her to guess how he'd spent those years.

'A few close brushes with the law put me in counselling. A last-ditch effort to save me from myself.'

And what? A possible jail sentence?

'It was there I came in contact with someone who cared, who talked the talk I understood. I had a knack with electronics. He put me in touch with a friend who presented me with an opportunity…and issued strict instructions I'd be out if I stuffed up.'

'You didn't.' That much was obvious, for he'd designed and patented a series of devices which attracted large companies worldwide. The rest became the mark by which legends were made.

'No.'

They shared a closeness that grew with each passing day. A bond she hugged close to her heart in the hope it might develop into *more.*

A cool breeze curled in from the ocean, and by tacit agreement they collected plates and flatware and retreated indoors to clear up.

It wasn't late, and Xavier dropped a kiss on top of her head. 'I'm flying into Sydney early tomorrow morning. Meetings that will run on to Tuesday.' He traced a forefinger over the fullness of her lower lip. 'Go slot in a DVD, and I'll join you soon.'

The DVD had reached the closing scene when he slid into a chair at her side, and he lifted her onto his lap as the credits rolled.

A hand cupped her breast and rested there before beginning a teasing circling motion that stirred alive her senses. A fact he knew very well, and she placed her lips against the edge of his jaw, nibbled a path to his earlobe…and nipped a little.

'You're insatiable.'

'Would you prefer it to be otherwise?'

Her answer was to cover his mouth with her own in a kiss that left no reason for doubt…and every need to seek their bed.

He was gentle, so incredibly gentle he almost brought her to tears, and afterwards she slept in his arms…only to wake in the morning to find she was alone in the bed.

Saying goodbye had been more difficult than Romy had imagined, and the imprint of Xavier's mouth as it had possessed her own stayed with her during the drive to school and much of the morning.

It was almost as if he'd found it hard to leave, and she held the thought close to her heart.

In bed…let's face it, *anywhere* they enjoyed sex, Xavier was everything she could wish for. Passionate, giving, primitive. Ensuring her emotional needs were met…and *more*.

Just *thinking* about the *more* melted her bones, and she issued a silent admonition to concentrate on the work, the students, the class.

Heaven forbid, he would only be away one night…it was not as if it was New York! So get a grip, why don't you?

Call Kassi, suggest dinner and a movie, a girlie night in watching DVDs.

Romy made the call during lunch break and set up a time

and place to meet, then, when the buzzer sounded over the address system announcing afternoon class, she collected her satchel and moved into the teachers' common room. It wasn't often she had a free break, and she intended to utilize it by marking Grade nine English homework assignments.

Ten minutes in, and she recollected the need to notify administration of a problem…something she could easily achieve with a phone call. Except it was a lovely early summer's day, the sun was shining, and she felt the need for some fresh air.

The walk to the administration block didn't take long, and she entered the main office, greeted the woman manning Reception, and stated her request.

A quick glance at the telephone communication system brought an apologetic smile. 'Suzy's on the phone in the back office. I'm sure she won't be long. Do you want to wait, or shall I have her call you?'

What did a few minutes matter? 'I'll wait.'

The phone rang, and Romy moved towards the notice-board, idly checking a few of the papers that had been push-pinned there. End-of-year exams were soon to begin, and the date and venue for the Grade twelve formal was up, together with various reminders of upcoming events.

The long summer break would herald a gap year for some whose parents could afford to send their teenager overseas before commencing university.

Romy vividly recalled her own gap year spent with a host family in Provence, where she'd polished her language skills and acquired a knowledge of French cuisine. A faint smile curved her lips…Paris in the spring time, she recalled, had spelt love in true romantic style, with an ardent French student who'd wooed her with wine and roses, picnics and sightseeing, Romy riding passenger on the back of his motorbike.

Friends, in the truest sense of the word.

A carefree time when life had been relatively simple, she mused in fond memory as she took a sideways step to read yet another notice.

Seconds later she sensed someone enter the office, and she turned slightly and glimpsed a male figure attired in jeans and a jacket whose hood partly obscured his facial features.

Something about him caused her instincts to go on alert. Deciphering body language was an art form, and one learnt well by those who taught children in school. A knowledge that, combined with finely tuned instinct, often prevented a situation from escalating out of control.

It kicked in now as she pretended further interest in the notice board, aware on a base level that she'd caught his attention.

The receptionist was occupied with an incoming call and gave no indication she'd noticed anything untoward. Yet all Romy's senses were heightened, and she attempted *calm* when every instinct warned her to leave *now*.

Oh, for heaven's sake, she dismissed in self-admonition. He's probably here on a mission, an older brother in lieu of a parent bent on communicating a message.

There was a sudden blur of movement, and he was there, in her face, a hand gripping her elbow in a killing grip as he shoved a hard object into her ribs. Dear heaven, what was that? A *gun?* Shock speared through her body at the possibility…although the logical part of her rationalized it was unlikely. Australia didn't have a 'right to bear arms' policy. Not that it prevented the illegal acquisition of a firearm.

'Walk.' The tone was guttural, decisive.

CHAPTER TWELVE

IT WAS PROBABLY a wasted effort to attempt to reason with her assailant, but it was worth a try.

'Do you really want to do this?' Romy kept her voice quiet, measured...only to have whatever he held in the pocket of his hoodie jammed so forcibly against her, it was almost impossible to stifle the gasp of pain that rose in her throat.

'Walk.'

Don't resist. A silent caution ensured she followed his terse instruction, and she saw the receptionist glance in their direction. One look was all it took, and her eyes widened as comprehension of the scene registered.

You and me, both, Romy agreed. Just...*don't panic.*

Unspoken words, but hopefully understood as her captor brought her to a halt in front of the reception desk.

'Money.'

The harsh directive sent the girl into shock, and any misgivings assumed a stark reality as he removed a hand from his pocket and brandished a hand gun.

'Money. *Now.*'

Damn. The silent expletive remained locked in her throat.

The girl seemed locked into immobility, and Romy uttered a silent plea...*just do as he says.*

The next instant hard metal lashed Romy's hand, and she groaned in pain.

'You're next,' he threatened the receptionist. *'Get the money.'*

That brought a result: the girl backed away, indicating a long *credenza* covering one wall. 'The safe is in there.'

'Open it and put all the cash in a bag.'

Please, God, let someone pass by, see what was in progress, and report it to the police.

Sure, and a police car would conveniently be in the next street. *Please.* By the time they received a call and arrived on the scene, the assailant would be long gone.

Unless someone disarmed him.

His attention was focused on the receptionist and the money she was removing from the safe.

If Romy was going to make a move, it had to be *now.*

With lightning quickness she swung her free hand down hard on his wrist in a karate chop her former instructor would have approved.

He screamed in pain as the gun clattered onto the floor, and she kicked it away out of his reach as he released his hold on her elbow to nurse his injured hand.

His rabid fury was fuelled by more than rage as he swung towards her and aimed a vicious kick…which she narrowly avoided by a hair's breadth as she automatically used his body weight against him and pinned him to the floor with a knee pressed against his spine.

People converged, together with the school's security guard, then the school principal.

It was then she had a good look at the assailant.

Young, still a teenager, Romy judged, with long, narrow facial features, hard eyes, and sporting a soul patch.

The gun was carefully bagged until the police arrived, and there was relief at the discovery it wasn't loaded.

Statements were taken, and an ambulance summoned despite Romy's protest she was fine to drive.

'Standard procedure for any injury in these circumstances,' a policewoman indicated and called on a school representative to pack the wrist with ice.

'A precaution, Romy,' the principal insisted. 'I'll ensure a call is placed to your home.'

'There's no need.'

'Nevertheless, the call will be made,' came the firm reply.

It seemed a case of definite overkill to ride in an ambulance, and she said so…only to have the driver reiterate the policewoman's words.

Hospital Accident & Emergency organized X-rays of her wrist, which thankfully showed only hairline fractures of three metacarpal bones. Her wrist was bound, painkillers dispensed, and while she waited for a taxi, she called Kassi and postponed dinner.

It was almost seven by the time she reached Brighton, and the instant the taxi drew to a halt adjacent to the front entrance, the door flew open, and Maria moved quickly to open the passenger door. 'Are you OK?'

The question held concern, and Romy offered her a reassuring smile as she paid off the driver. 'I'm fine. Just a badly bruised wrist.'

'Your Mini is in the garage,' Maria revealed. 'The school arranged it. Tea,' the housekeeper insisted as they entered the foyer. 'A strong cup of sweet tea, then you will eat.'

'Bossy,' Romy said with a smile, and the housekeeper shook her head.

'Not nearly as bossy as your husband will be.'

Xavier. Romy closed her eyes, then opened them again. 'Please tell me you didn't contact him.'

'Not to do so would be more than my employment is worth.'

Well, that meant relaying a *guess what happened yesterday* anecdote when he returned tomorrow evening wasn't going to happen!

Dammit, she'd kept her cellphone on mute during class, and given the afternoon's events she hadn't thought to check it for messages.

Something she attended to immediately and discovered there were several. Three from Xavier, demanding she call him, two from Kassi wanting an update, and one from the principal, with his home number for her to call.

Romy made the calls in reverse order and provided suitable reassurance…except Xavier's phone carried an automated message, and she simply left a 'returning your call' on his message bank.

There was nothing he could do. Two more painkillers when she went to bed, followed by a good night's sleep and she'd feel almost normal in the morning.

Romy drank the tea Maria prepared and ate a small portion of food, then she pleaded the need for a shower and change of clothes.

'Do you need some help?' the housekeeper queried with concern, and Romy shook her head.

'Thanks. I'll be able to manage.'

It was something of a relief to enter the master suite, and she toed off her shoes, removed her clothes, and decided on a bath. A leisurely soak held appeal, and she filled the large tub, added bath oil, placed her cellphone within reach, then she sank down into the scented depths with a pleasurable sigh.

The afternoon's events replayed through her mind, and she wondered how it would have played out if she hadn't taken affirmative action. Unless she was mistaken, her assailant had been under the influence of an illegal substance and therefore his actions had been unpredictable at best.

Don't think about it. There was no point.

The sudden peal of her cellphone had her reaching for it, and Xavier's name showed on caller ID. 'Hi.'

'Right back at you.'

The sound of his voice caused her toes to curl, together with a reaction in other intimate parts of her body.

'I tried to ring you, but it went to message bank,' Romy explained.

Due to the fact he had been making calls to the hospital, the school, organizing a flight, Xavier refrained from revealing.

Did she have any idea how Maria's call had affected him? The volatile mix of anger and fear…with the accent on *fear*. Not so much what had happened, but just how bad it could have been?

Dammit, *he could have lost her.*

Little fool. Taking on a young idiot high on drugs in possession of a gun.

Mierda. His blood ran cold at the mere thought.

'I'm fine.'

She possessed an inner strength that was admirable, but it hid a tender heart and a degree of vulnerability she managed to cover too well.

'Uh-huh.'

'You're angry.'

You have no idea. Except he bit back the words. 'We need to talk.' And they would, *soon.*

'OK.'

He sensed the tentative reserve in her voice and managed a faint smile.

'So how was your day?'

He almost laughed. *Almost.* 'About to get better.'

'I guess you're dining with colleagues.'

Xavier entered the bedroom, shrugged out of his jacket and tossed it onto a nearby chair. Then he loosened his tie, toed off his shoes, removed his socks, set down his cell-phone…and crossed to the *en suite.*

Romy gasped as the door swung open, her eyes wide with a mix of shock, surprise…and something else she couldn't begin to define.

'What are you doing here?' The words escaped before she could give them thought. If it were possible, her eyes widened further as she saw him pull free his tie and then begin releasing the buttons on his shirt.

His eyes never left her own. 'You imagined I'd remain in Sydney?'

Well…*yes.* 'There was no need for you to come back,' she said quietly, and attempted to tamp down the spiralling emotion arcing through her body as he removed his shirt.

'You think not?'

His breadth of shoulder, the superb muscle definition caused the breath to hitch in her throat as he reached for the belt fastening his trousers, and her mouth parted as he slid free the zip.

'What are you doing?' The query sounded slightly strangled, even to her own ears.

'Sharing your bath.' He stepped out of his trousers, then he unfastened his watch and placed it on the marble vanity.

'I'm fine.' The words scarcely left her lips as he cradled her head between his hands and closed his mouth over her own in an evocative salutation that tore the breath from her throat.

She was unaware of time or place as she gave herself up to the sensual caress of his tongue as he explored the sensitive tissues in a need to stamp his possession.

When he lifted his head, she could only look at him wordlessly.

'Really?' Xavier posed with deliberate quiet. His eyes speared her own as he released her and skimmed his hands down his hips, taking his silk briefs with them, and he stepped into the scented water to settle facing her.

His eyes were dark, slumbrous and intense with an expression she was hesitant to divine as he carefully brought her injured hand to his lips.

'I've heard the official version,' he offered calmly. 'Now I want yours. From the beginning.'

'While we're in the bath?'

'It's where you are.'

Why did simple logic sound so…expressive. Or was he just playing the caring husband?

He looked…larger than life, wholly male, and his close proximity in such intimate surroundings affected the beat of her heart, quickening and thickening it so she almost *felt* its reverberating thud in every pulse throughout her body.

His hands shaped her shoulders, slid to each elbow, then moved to her ribs, and his eyes narrowed as her breath caught as he explored the slight swelling there.

His eyes seared hers. 'Romy?'

'I'm sure the official version covered everything.'

'Not quite. There are gaps.'

He didn't intend to let up, she could tell. Which left little option but to relay a brief account, unaware her expressive features conveyed more than mere words ever could.

'That's it,' she concluded with a careless shrug.

Not quite, he reflected, but it was enough for now, and he watched her eyes dilate as he cupped her cheek and soothed a thumb over the soft skin.

'What made you think you could disarm him?' His tone was even, calm...when he'd died a thousand deaths over the past few hours imagining a different outcome.

'The opportunity was there, and I took it,' she managed with forced insouciance and saw a muscle clench at the edge of his jaw.

'*Dammit,* Romy.' He bit back a vicious oath. 'What were you thinking? He had a gun.'

She resorted to defence. 'It wasn't loaded.'

His eyes became almost black. 'You couldn't have known that.'

Should she mention this episode wasn't the first? That combat skills had formed an integral part of extra-curricular training for those who taught at her previous school...where she'd suffered a fractured clavicle, con-cussion, and other minor injuries during her three-year stint there?

Although perhaps now wasn't the time. At this particu-lar moment she was sufficiently intrigued by his concern. And the reason *why.*

Could it mean he *cared?* Perhaps have become emotion-ally attached to her? Something *more*...deeper than just the enjoyment of very good sex?

Hope unfurled deep inside, and she contained it out of fear she might be wrong.

Instead, she reached out her unbound hand and traced a finger over a visible scar that crossed a jagged path across his ribs.

'You have a few battle scars of your own.' Each of which

she'd brushed with her lips, and she inwardly ached as she wondered at whatever situation had caused them.

His eyes darkened further, almost as if he read her thought pattern. 'There's a vast difference.'

Romy held his gaze. 'Is there?'

A thousand-fold, he admitted silently. His fight had been for survival in a place he had no wish to revisit. Where a switchblade could do irreparable harm, knuckledusters maim and disfigure, and the vicious use of nunchucks and chains could kill...and did.

It had shaped who he was at that time, created the drive and perspicacity to hone his wits in order to escape.

And he had, clawing his way by means that didn't bear close scrutiny as he took every edge and turned it to his advantage...building his future with a ruthlessness he knew to be legend. Yet it had gained him reluctant respect among his peers and aided the amassing of a fortune.

Much of his past remained a closed book, with only the barest of details discovered by the media over time.

Yet the mystique remained, and there were those who added conjecture to purported fact...labelling him as a man to regard with caution. A fact he'd learnt to accept with a degree of silent amusement.

'Yes.'

Succinct, and bare of details Romy doubted he'd choose to share.

She had a need to put some space between them, to remove herself from an evocative situation where the current direction could tip her into unchartered territory. And she'd had enough confrontation for the day.

'I'm done.' She made to rise to her feet, only to have Xavier curl a hand over her shoulder.

'Except I'm far from done.'

Romy shot him a slightly desperate look.

'Stay,' he bade her quietly, and she was held mesmerized by his expression for a few heart-stopping seconds, then she gasped out loud as he lifted her legs over his thighs and brought her close.

So close she couldn't help but be aware of his arousal, and she looked at him quesioningly, only to have him give a slight shake of his head as he lowered his head to savour the sweet curve at the edge of her neck.

Sensation, violently sweet, shivered through her body at his touch, and, unbidden, she arched her head to allow him access.

His hands cupped her breasts as he explored their shape and texture, and a faint groan escaped her lips when he teased each tender peak into a hardened nub.

Not content, he trailed a hand down to her waist and traced her navel before moving low as he sought and found the sensitive folds.

Oh, my God.

This…*this* was almost more than she could bear, and the breath caught in her throat as he inserted one finger in an exploratory foray that locked her gaze with his.

Eyes, dark with sin, flared as he sent her high, and she cried out as she felt the telltale spiral soar with primal need to a peak where he held her for timeless seconds before she tipped over the edge in glorious free fall.

Then his mouth possessed her own, with a gentleness that almost brought her to tears, and she whimpered, wanting, *needing* more…so much more.

All of him…body, mind and soul. *His.*

He knew…dear lord, how could he not?

She was beyond thought, so distanced from everything

except the man and the electric sensuality that fused them together as one.

Did she plead with him? She only knew she wanted to, and she gasped out loud as he rose to his feet, scooped her carefully into his arms and stepped out from the bath.

He took a towel and gently dried the moisture from her body, then he tended to his own, and she stood locked into immobility as he held her gaze until he was done.

In one fluid movement he placed an arm beneath her knees and carried her into the bedroom, and, reaching the large bed, he tugged the covers down, then carefully lowered her onto the sheets before joining her there.

With unhurried grace he propped his elbow to support his head in one hand, and trailed gentle fingers over the swell of her breasts. The breath hissed through his teeth as he caught sight of the burgeoning bruise on her ribcage, and he traced it carefully before lowering his head to place his lips there.

Seduction…he was so *good* at it, Romy acknowledged tremulously as he caressed each pleasure pulse with languorous warmth.

It became a slow and delicious torture until she reached a sensual conflagration, and there was only one word she could utter…*now.*

He obliged, moving over her body as he eased his impressive length in a slow slide to the hilt, held it there as her muscles clenched around him…then he began to move, gently at first, his dark eyes capturing her own as pulsing need consumed her.

Yet it was he who governed the pace, resisting her plea to go faster, harder, as he finessed the loving, and he took possession of her mouth, capturing her cries as he led her high with such care she was moved to tears.

He felt the liquid warmth as they seeped down her cheeks, and he shifted his mouth to gently absorb them.

An act which only caused them to flow more freely.

'Dios,' Xavier cursed softly, and he lifted his head; his eyes were dark as they met her own. 'Did I hurt you?'

She shook her head. He'd been so careful not to.

Sex, even very good sex, didn't necessarily mean he *cared.* So get a grip and pass on the emotional evaluation.

She was his *wife.* This afternoon she'd become involved in something newsworthy. How would it have looked if he hadn't rushed to her side?

'Amante,' he began silkily. 'You imagine I don't care if anything happens to you?' He moved, rolling carefully onto his back, taking her with him as he positioned her back against his bent knees. 'Why do you think I walked out of a meeting and took the first flight home?'

'You couldn't wait to check the damage to your physical asset?'

He wanted to wring her delicate little neck. Instead he cupped her face and brought her down within touching distance…and kissed her. Thoroughly.

When he was done, he traced her slightly swollen mouth with a gentle finger. 'You sweet fool.' He smiled…an expression that brought warmth to his dark eyes and softened his chiselled features.

'How can you doubt it? I adore everything you are. The way your body seeks mine in the dark of night. Your generosity. How you stand up for what you believe in.' He paused and trailed light fingers across her cheek. 'All of it…and more.'

Care was good. *Adore* was even better. Except it wasn't *love*…the ultimate emotion in its simplest truth, from his heart, his soul.

'You once said you didn't do love.'

'Because I'd never had it,' Xavier revealed. 'And failed to recognize the gift until you walked away from me.'

Romy remained silent, absorbing his words and the many unanswered questions.

'Nothing to say, *querida?*'

Her eyes resembled dark sapphires, deep enough for a man to drown in.

'Yet you went to great lengths to make any contact with you almost impossible.'

He didn't pretend to misunderstand. 'Anger with your father for placing himself, and therefore *you,* in such an invidious position.' No one defrauded him...no one.

'You could have insisted on reinstating me as your mistress. It would have been much simpler. Instead, you offered a solution that bordered on blackmail.'

'I wanted you as my wife.' He paused imperceptibly. 'Legally bound and sharing my name.'

She'd started down this dangerous path. Now she had to play it out to the end.

'And the insistence I bear you a child?'

'Leverage,' he admitted. 'With the knowledge you could never abandon a child of your own. Our child.' He waited a beat, his eyes impossibly dark. 'I live in the hope you will eventually consider pregnancy.'

Her eyes widened, and she opened her mouth, only to close it again. 'You don't use protection.'

'You think it didn't occur to me you might take the pill as an act of defiance in order to retain a measure of control?'

Whatever had made her believe she could fool him? He knew all the angles, every twist and turn of the human mind.

She swallowed the sudden lump that rose in her throat. 'I hated you for making that condition.'

'Among others.'

'Yes,' she reproved fiercely…aware it didn't quite hit the mark, for things had changed. Changes that almost came full circle. Almost, but not quite.

Xavier lifted her easily and settled her down at his side, then tucked her head into the curve of his shoulder.

The warmth of his smile seeped beneath her skin and into her bones.

'Sleep easy, *mi mujer.*' He brushed his lips to her forehead. 'And know I hold you through the night.'

She felt a degree of peace and security, each of which would have been absent had she been alone. She wanted to thank him for being here for her, except she slid into blissful oblivion before she could utter the words.

CHAPTER THIRTEEN

THE sun's warm fingers were filtering through the closed shutters when Romy woke, and a quick glance was all it took to determine she was alone in the bed.

There was no sound to indicate Xavier occupied the shower, and she quickly checked her watch, muttered an unladylike oath at the time and hit the shower running. Conscious, as she did so, of a degree of pain...her wrist, ribs. Everything took a little longer, and she cursed afresh at the awkwardness resulting from needing to protect her wrist.

It was almost eight when she entered the kitchen, where Maria greeted her in surprise.

'Good morning. Xavier has already left for the city, and he said not to disturb you.'

'It's a weekday. I have school.' It would take much worse than an injured hand to prevent her attendance! 'I need to be there,' Romy said quietly and met the housekeeper's doubtful look.

'Do you think that's wise?'

Wisdom had little to do with it, and she said so.

'How is your hand?'

Sore. But painkillers with her coffee would soon take the edge off. 'OK.' An ambiguous answer, if ever there was one, but it was all she'd admit to as she took a tub of yoghurt from the refrigerator, added a banana, took a piece of toast and ate standing at the kitchen servery.

Driving didn't pose a problem, although leaving later than usual meant she encountered more traffic, and she entered the teachers' common room to be greeted by fellow staff members who expressed collective concern.

It gave her a warm feeling, brightened the morning, and she emerged in order to reach her classroom ahead of time.

There was a need to check the day's curriculum, and she was almost there when one of her female students crossed the hallway to command her attention.

A pretty girl, petite in stature and blonde. A good student, Romy recalled, who, the records revealed, had entered the school's system at the beginning of the year after settling in Sydney from Washington, USA.

'Suzy. You wanted to speak with me?'

'Are you OK?' The girl seemed overly anxious. 'I mean, *really* OK?'

'I'm fine.'

'It would be uncool if anything happened to you.' There was a pause, then Suzy rushed on, 'You're my role model.' She gave a soundless gulp, then the words began pouring out of her. 'You're new, and being new can be not so great. A friend saw me slip a note into your satchel and told my mom, who made me 'fess up and said I had to tell you and apologize, cos you could report it.' She took in a deep breath and released it. 'I'm sorry. Please don't file a report,' she begged. 'I didn't mean any harm. I only wanted you to know you're a fab teacher.'

Romy hid her relief. A mystery solved, innocent with no ill intent.

'That's a nice compliment.' Now to convey an element

of caution. 'However, anonymous notes can cause suspicion.'

The girl looked suitably remorseful. 'I didn't mean to alarm you.' The possibility she might have done so, brought forth a heartfelt apology. 'I'm so sorry. *Really* sorry.' For a moment she looked stricken. 'You're not angry? I couldn't bear it if you were angry with me.'

Oh, hell. There was a little too much emotion going on here. 'Teachers want the best for their students, and it's good to learn their teaching skills are appreciated.'

'Just not via anonymous notes.'

'No.'

Suzy's face cleared a little. 'You won't report me?'

'Consider you've received a warning this time. Just don't do it again.'

'Thank you…you're the best.'

At that moment the buzzer sounded, announcing assembly in the main hall, where, once the students were gathered together, the principal conducted a debriefing associated with the previous day's attempted robbery, then he dismissed them to their various classrooms and motioned Romy to one side.

'I spoke to your husband early this morning, and we agreed you should take the rest of the week off.'

We? She doubted the 'we'…only Xavier's influence.

'My husband,' she said carefully, 'should have checked with me first. I don't require any time off.'

'Nevertheless, I've arranged for another teacher to take your classes, starting tomorrow.' He sought to provide reassurance. 'You were exceedingly brave yesterday, and your action undoubtedly prevented a bad situation from becoming much worse. Consider the time off as a form of thanks from the school board.'

To refuse would be churlish, and she thanked him.

'A pleasure.'

The temptation to call Xavier and demand an explanation was uppermost, but she was due in class. Overdue, she realized as she checked her watch.

The morning assumed its normal pattern, and it wasn't until lunch break that Romy checked her cellphone. Two messages…one from Xavier, another from Kassi, and a message from her father.

She spoke to Kassi first, then hit Xavier's private number.

'You're at school?' He knew, damn him. The silky voice curled round her heart and tugged a little, for it conjured up images of their shared bath, his mind-blowing ministrations.

She aimed for a light-hearted response and didn't quite make it. 'What made you think I wouldn't be?'

'Your stubborn-mindedness.' She could sense the slight edge of amusement in his drawled response.

'I prefer to call it dedication.'

'I'll look forward to continuing this discussion tonight.'

'There's nothing further to discuss.'

'You think not? *Buenos dias,* Romy.'

Sexy, she thought. *Very.* And she got to go home to him.

Last night he'd said the *adore* word…causing her a momentary lack of speech. Were they merely words motivated by the moment? She'd been too afraid to ask.

Yet even during their live-in relationship, it had been a word he'd never uttered…not once. And she'd hungered for it, wanting, needing the verbal confirmation of what she thought they shared.

Was it possible he'd changed? There was a part of her that longed to believe he had.

The afternoon classes drew to a close, and Romy collected her satchel, then she drove home, called her father, showered and changed into jeans and a top, took some fruit and bottled water from the kitchen, and settled down in the bedroom to mark homework assignments.

It was there Xavier found her, and he stood for a moment, noting her level of concentration, the reading glasses that had slid part-way down her pert little nose…the way she bit her lip when a student resorted to idioms instead of grammar.

She was something else. *His.* In a way no other woman could ever be.

He saw the moment she sensed his presence, and he crossed the room to her side, placed a thumb and finger beneath her chin and brushed her mouth with his own, then he queried lightly, 'How was your day?'

A smile curved his lips as she pushed her glasses up onto her head and regarded him steadily. 'Fine. And yours?'

He shrugged off his jacket and loosened his tie. 'Conference calls, meetings. The usual.' He discarded his tie and undid the top few buttons of his shirt. 'Shouldn't you be resting that hand?'

She merely gave an expressive eye roll as she leant back in the chair. 'Two things,' she began and earned his arched eyebrow.

'Only two?'

'You had no right to organize for me to have the rest of the week off. I'm capable of making my own decisions.'

She watched as he removed his cufflinks and rolled back his sleeves. His movements were studied, and his eyes seared her own as he moved close to cage her body with a hand either side of her chair.

'And the other thing?'

He was too close, his proximity too dangerous to her peace of mind, and she felt the familiar warmth invade her body, heating it with languorous sensual need.

'The notes slid among the homework assignments were

harmless,' she revealed as she made a conscious effort to still her rapidly beating pulse. 'One of the students confessed they were merely intended as a compliment.'

'You believe it?'

'Yes,' she said without hesitation.

Xavier lifted a hand, removed the glasses perched on top of her head and placed them on the side pedestal. 'Come share my shower.'

'You only want to get me naked.'

His soft chuckle almost undid her. 'That, too.'

'We'll be late for dinner.'

'So we'll be late.'

Romy's eyes took on an impish gleam. 'What if I'm hungry...for food?'

His mouth twitched with humour. 'You're enjoying this, aren't you?'

'Uh-huh.'

He cupped the side of her face, tilted it a little, then brushed his mouth to her own. 'Two can play, *querida*. I'll take a shower, we'll eat, then—'

'View a DVD?'

A soft laugh escaped his lips. 'Delay the anticipation? I can manage.' He moved across the room and turned as he reached the en suite. 'Will you?'

'Easily.'

She tried, she really did. But her focus for marking assignments went out the window as she became consumed by Xavier's naked image. The tall, superbly muscled frame, the expanse of tanned skin marred in places by scars whose history he steadfastly refused to reveal. The tight butt, and his masculine attributes.

Don't go there...although the vivid memory taunted her, turning the blood in her veins to liquid fire.

So why delay the moment?

Because she'd been wrong three years ago, she acknowledged. What if she was wrong *now?*

What if he was merely lulling her into a comfort zone where she accepted they could share a fulfilling life together? That a few words of affection and very good sex was *enough?*

He was, after all, *Xavier DeVasquez,* self-made billionaire…any number of women would happily settle for less just to bear his name and share his fortune.

Why couldn't *she?*

Because none of it mattered…except the man himself. His heart, his soul. Gifted freely, with no strings attached.

She didn't hear him re-enter the bedroom, nor did she witness his slightly narrowed gaze as he crossed to her side.

'Put the work away,' he said quietly. 'And we'll go eat.'

Maria had fixed a delicious meal, with a vanilla sorbet and fresh fruit for dessert.

Romy tried to do the food justice, but there were questions for which she needed answers. Questions she was hesitant to ask in case the answers were not what she wanted to hear.

One issue, however, figured largely in her mind, and she voiced it as she pushed her plate to one side.

'I intend to go to school tomorrow.'

Xavier regarded her carefully as he replaced his flatware. 'It's not going to happen.'

'Excuse me?'

'We're flying to Lizard Island in the morning for a four-day break.'

Lizard Island was an exclusive luxury resort situated north of Cairns in Far North Queensland.

'That's impossible.'

'Nothing is impossible, *querida.*'

His presence dominated the room, and she stood to her feet in a bid to be free of him, gathering plates and flatware together, and carrying them through to the kitchen where she proceeded to rinse and stack the dishwasher.

He followed in her wake, and she was achingly aware of him as he disposed of leftovers with ease of movement, finishing the task in unison with her.

For a few seconds her gaze locked with his, and she was disarmed by his smile.

'You mentioned viewing a DVD?'

It was on the tip of her tongue to say she'd changed her mind. She was tired…not sleepy-tired, but so consumed with conflicting emotions she craved solitude. And if they were to leave early in the morning, she should pack.

Yet, conversely, she didn't want to retire to the bedroom. For it was there she came undone.

All it took was the brush of his hand, his lips…and she lost all rational thought.

'Yes. The movie had good reviews,' she managed quietly. 'I missed seeing it in a cinema.'

'Then let's go watch it, hmm?'

The media room, with its plush leather recliner seating, large screen and soft lighting, provided a private, intimate home cinema, and Romy retrieved the DVD, slotted it into the player, then settled into a comfortable chair while Xavier used a remote to dim the lights.

The actors were superb in the parts they portrayed, the plot quirky and electrifying, and the last thing she remembered was a terrifying car chase through the streets of San Francisco…the spectacular resolution of which she missed.

At one point, Xavier carefully shifted her from the chair

onto his lap and tucked her head into the curve of his shoulder…where he kept her until the DVD ended, before taking her to their bed—to sleep.

CHAPTER FOURTEEN

THE TROPICAL WATERS gleamed a translucent green above coral beds as the Hinterland flight transfer from Cairns began its descent onto Lizard Island.

Powdery white sand covered the various-shaped coves and small promontories, and provided a contrast to the dark green shrubbery.

An island paradise frequented by the wealthy, catering to those who enjoyed tranquility, pampering, fine food and wine in luxurious surroundings…at a price. A place where visitors came to relax and unwind, away from the hype and buzz of the city, and the cares of a stressful lifestyle.

It was beautiful, Romy noted as they were met, greeted, and delivered with friendly deference to their Sunset Point accommodation…one of a few villas set high on a ridge offering sea views filtered through native bushland.

Polished timber floors, an outside deck with chairs and a hammock, and stylish modern furniture and amenities graced their villa, and Romy executed a graceful turn as Xavier took care of their bags.

'I love it here,' she said with sparkling enthusiasm. 'One could easily become an indolent sybarite without any effort at all.'

Casual wear, Xavier had advised as she'd rushed to pack before they'd left early that morning, and she'd slipped a bikini and swimsuit, with matching sarong, shorts, a pair of tailored trousers and two tops, jeans and a sweatshirt in case the evenings grew cool, trainers, together with personal items into her bag.

Consequently, unpacking took very little time, and when it was done, Romy tucked her hand in his and tugged him towards the door.

'Let's go explore.'

Magic, she thought as they walked down onto the beach. It was easy to slip off her trainers and walk barefoot in the sand. Impossible not to paddle along the foreshore, and she laughed as Xavier followed suit.

There was a relaxed, comfortable feeling between them as he curved an arm along the back of her waist, and a warm chuckle escaped from his lips when she kicked a playful splash of water against his legs.

'I should take you to task.'

'Threat or promise?'

It was almost as if they were turning back the clock, and Romy tilted her head and let it rest briefly against his shoulder. 'Thank you.'

'For what, specifically?'

'Bringing me here.'

He dropped a light kiss onto the top of her head. 'My pleasure.'

Did wishes come true? Sometimes, if you believed in them. And if so, was true happiness too much to ask?

It was almost dusk when they returned to their villa, where they showered, changed and walked down to the dining room for dinner.

Dimmed lights, moonlight painting a gleaming path on the water, fine food…what more could anyone ask?

A waiter served coffee, and Xavier settled back in his chair.

'We'll take a catamaran out in the morning. The coral beds are worth seeing.'

No work, no battling peak-hour traffic. Homework assignments wouldn't exist for a few days. An idyllic setting…*and* she got to spend twenty-four seven with her husband.

'Would you like to cross into the lounge?'

Mix and mingle? Attempt to have a conversation against background music and the chatter of fellow guests? Besides, there was a wedding reception happening, so she shook her head. 'Let's take a walk along the beach in the moonlight.'

His warm smile held a degree of amusement. 'You want romance?'

'Just…you.'

It was nice. Really nice, to enjoy the peaceful surroundings, the solitude, and the vast emptiness of the night's ocean. An awareness the world…the world as they knew it, was far away.

Neither spoke as they walked hand-in-hand in a circuitous route back to their villa, and once inside Romy melted into his arms, lifting her head to welcome his kiss. Lingering, when she wanted passion, and it was Xavier who gently put her at arm's length and reached for a slim pictorial folder on a nearby table.

'You might like to check this out.'

She accepted it with a musing smile. 'What have you done?'

'Open the brochure.'

She did, and it brought a pleased gasp to her lips.

Concurrent spa treatments the following afternoon…for each of them. Sheer bliss, and she gave a delighted smile. 'Thank you.'

In a natural progression she reached for his shirt buttons and slowly released each one…and laughed a little as he returned the favour.

Undressing became a slow, evocative tease, with the light brush of her fingers, the sensual kiss he bestowed on the hollow at the edge of her neck. And when the last vestige of clothing slid to the timbered floor, they indulged in an erotic feast of the senses until only intimacy would suffice.

It was then Xavier tossed the bedcovers aside and drew her down onto the sheets, where their lovemaking ignited a shimmering passion that soared high as it encompassed mind, body and spirit…theirs, in a primitive, almost pagan unison that transcended anything they'd previously shared.

More, so much more than very good sex, Romy accepted as her heartbeat gradually slowed to a regular beat. Infinitely special.

Love. She almost said the words. Heard the words he uttered in Spanish…only to fail with the translation, and she fell into an exhausted sleep before she could ask him.

The next morning they woke early, donned casual wear and took a long walk along the beach. The cool waters were a translucent green, the surface dappled beneath the rising warmth of a tropical sun, and there was a sense of tranquility. A shared silence that obviated the need for conversation.

Simple pleasures, Romy mused as they eventually made their way to the dining room and selected breakfast from the buffet.

Fresh juice, aromatic coffee, and delicious food. It was a wonderful beginning to a delightful day.

Taking the catamaran out proved spectacular, with the

craft skimming over the water, the light breeze ruffled her hair while her exposed skin took on a sun-kissed glow.

There was time for a quick shower, followed by a light lunch eaten alfresco before checking in to the spa for their afternoon treatments.

Heaven. Simply heaven to lie supine on soft warm towels and be indulged and nurtured by signature therapies designed to soothe and enhance the skin and body. Beneath the hands of a skilled masseuse it was impossible not to relax and simply enjoy the incredible sense of peace.

One could, Romy perceived dreamily, easily become accustomed to such luxury on a regular basis!

'Good?' Xavier queried as they emerged from the spa fully dressed, and her mouth curved into a delicious smile.

'*Wonderful* doesn't begin to cover it.' Her eyes sparkled with pleasure as he looped an arm along the back of her waist.

He looked relaxed, almost contented, and she spared him a curious glance as he indicated a path leading down to the beach.

There was an earthiness in walking barefoot along the soft powdery sand, almost a silent commune with nature as they wandered arm-in-arm towards the water's edge and headed towards a distant low rocky promontory.

When they reached it, Romy expected him to turn and head back, except he sank down on a nearby flat rock and drew her to stand between his thighs.

Her eyes widened as he cradled her face and closed his mouth over hers in a gentle kiss that made her want to lean in and deepen the contact.

The faint scent of the subtle oil used by the masseuse lingered, warmly sensual as he used each thumb-pad to smooth a light path down the edge of her throat, and she became conscious of each pulse deepening to a thudding beat.

There was a sense of loss as he lifted his head, and her eyes dilated at the dark warmth apparent in his own. The edges of his mouth curved a little into a languorous smile.

'Will you share the rest of your life with me?' Xavier queried gently and glimpsed her momentary uncertainty.

'I thought that was the plan.'

'Mine,' he agreed quietly. 'But not yours, initially.'

Was this a time for truth? To confront past issues and hopefully resolve them? 'No,' she admitted. 'I hated you for what you did.'

Her honesty brought an bemused quirk to the edge of his lips. 'And now?'

Dared she go for broke? Bare her heart, her soul? 'Not so much.'

'Would it help if I said I love you?'

She felt her mouth tremble, and her eyes widened into deep sapphire pools as he eased the pad of his thumb over her lower lip.

'Only if you mean it.'

'Unequivocally,' he assured her gently. 'Beyond reason.'

It was so what she wanted to hear, yet words temporarily failed her.

'I imagined myself to be immune.' A faint smile teased the corners of his mouth. 'A hardened cynic in total control of his emotions. Or so I thought,' he owned quietly. 'Until you entered my life.' His eyes became dark with passion. 'And filled it with light. And love,' he added. 'Except I was a fool, and you walked.'

'Ran,' Romy amended. 'As far and as fast as I could. Because to stay, to catch so much as an inadvertent glimpse of you with someone else would have killed me.'

'No one came close,' he admitted. 'They weren't *you*.' He traced a light finger over her lower lip. 'Then fate intervened when Andre's accounting aroused suspicion, which eventually became proven, and charges were laid.'

'And you involved me in a diabolical game.'

'A calculated manoeuvre,' Xavier corrected. 'One that would put you in my hands and keep you there…for a while. A place where I hoped to persuade you to stay.'

'I think,' Romy managed quietly. 'I need to hear you say it again.'

Xavier's eyes trapped hers and held her mesmerized at the depth of passion evident. 'I love you,' he vowed gently. 'You…only you.' His lips brushed hers, settled a little, then lifted mere centimetres. 'You're my life, the reason I exist.' He paused a beat. 'Beyond doubt.'

'Yes.' It was such a simple word, but it meant so much. 'I'll stay. For the rest of my life.'

His eyes gentled with an emotion that captured her heart and made it *his*…completely, without reservation.

For a heart-stopping moment it appeared he wasn't capable of uttering so much as a word, and she wound her arms round his neck and pressed her mouth to his in a kiss that conveyed so much more than mere words ever could.

'*Gracias.*' His voice was husky with barely controlled passion, and her bones melted beneath the warmth of his smile as he positioned her head against the curve of his shoulder.

'I need to make a call.'

'Important?' Romy teased and felt his lips settle briefly on her forehead.

'Uh-huh.'

It was a short conversation, she reflected dreamily as he pocketed his cellphone.

'Let's go.'

'To dinner?'

Xavier rose to his feet and looped an arm around her shoulders. 'Eventually.'

Her mouth curved to form a teasing smile. 'You have something planned?'

'You could say that.'

Making love. Just the mere thought sent the blood fizzing through her veins and set each separate nerve end quivering with sensual heat. It was then she'd show him how much he meant to her and voice the words she wanted to say.

From that moment on, they'd share a new beginning. One where there were no secrets, no lingering recriminations. Only deep, abiding love.

She became misty-eyed and sensed his swift glance.

'Hey,' he chided her gently, and she offered him a tear-drenched smile.

'A girl is allowed some emotional reaction.'

It was amazing, Romy mused as they reached the path leading to their villa, how the sun seemed a little brighter, the day more beautiful in every way.

The excitement built as Xavier unlocked their door, then ushered her inside.

The scene she'd vividly imagined was so fixed in her mind, she failed in those first few seconds to register that the main room was different from the way it had been when they'd left.

For one thing, a staff member moved forward to greet her.

'Good afternoon, Romy. My name is Michelle, and I'm here to assist you.'

To do what? 'I'm sorry, I don't understand,' she said, genuinely perplexed, and she turned slightly. 'Xavier?'

He placed a hand at the back of her waist and smoothed

it up to her nape in a gentle gesture. 'We have an appointment in an hour with a celebrant for a reaffirmation of our wedding vows.' He indicated two dress bags hanging from a mobile luggage trolley. 'Michelle will help you dress.'

His words rendered her speechless as she met the lazy amusement apparent in his gaze.

'The resort staff have kindly made another villa available for my use.' He dropped a light kiss to her cheek. 'I'll be back soon.'

'We should get started,' Michelle said kindly the instant the door closed behind him.

They did, with Michelle issuing suggestions Romy merely followed…unsure when *stunned* changed to warm and fuzzy excitement.

She took the quickest shower on record, then, towelled dry, she emerged into the bedroom to discover a beautiful full-length wedding gown spread out on the king-size bed. Together with everything a bride could need…right down to gorgeous ivory stilettos, stunning underwear, a fingertip veil, and bouquet.

'The hair first, next make-up, then the dress,' Michelle detailed, indicating a chair, and Romy slid into it with a smile.

'You've done this before.'

'How did you guess?' came the impish response as she got to work.

The end result was…*magic*. Romy not only looked bridal, she felt like a bride. The gown was perfect in style and fit, ditto the stilettos, and she turned as Xavier re-entered the room, saw the way he looked at her…and melted.

This, *this* was a moment she'd treasure for the rest of her life. The passion, *love*…there, clearly evident in his expression. For her.

He moved towards her, tall, dark, resplendent in impeccable tailoring, snowy white shirt and black tie.

When he reached her, he trailed light fingers down her cheek, and he gently complimented her—'Beautiful.' He smiled, and she met it with one of her own. 'Ready?'

She'd never been more ready in her life. 'Yes.'

Xavier indicated the path leading down to the beach, and Romy looked at him in silent wonder as they reached a private marquee set with a table covered in fine damask. A celebrant waited, together with two witnesses, and, introductions complete, the intimate ceremony began.

Romy was completely charmed by the spoken words so warmly delivered, making it very personal...*special.*

Because this time they both spoke vows with love.

There was an ethereal feeling as the sun lowered in the sky, changing from red to saffron, then pink as dusk descended.

Two votive candles provided light as Xavier slid a magnificent square-cut diamond ring onto her finger, and her mouth trembled as he lifted her hand to his lips in a silent, intimate salute.

It was incredibly touching, and his eyes darkened measurably as she returned the gesture.

There was only him, the tall, broad-framed man who represented her world. The celebrant, the two witnesses faded from her vision, and she was barely conscious of voicing her polite thanks as she accepted their congratulations and good wishes.

Then they were alone, and they stood together in mutual silence, savouring the moment, the fading light and the emergence of the moon as it cast a milky glow.

Being here with him encapsulated everything she could wish for, and she leant in against him, felt his answering warmth, the light touch of his lips against her forehead.

A light switched on above the table, and soft music filtered through hidden speakers as waitstaff delivered champagne and a series of covered dishes.

Dinner.

Romy didn't feel as if she could eat a thing, but the various aromas proved tempting, and she sampled the starter, then accepted a morsel Xavier offered from his plate.

It became a slow seduction of the senses as they fed each other food and sampled superb French champagne. She felt complete, as if everything in her life had led to this moment.

It was a while before they rose and wandered back to their villa.

There was a need to thank him…and she did, her expressive features more eloquent than the words she offered.

'You did this for me,' she added quietly as he closed the door behind them.

'Everything I do is for you.'

Love…*his* for her, was there, clearly and unashamedly evident for her to see.

She felt her eyes fill with tears, and she blinked hard to prevent their flow, but one wayward tear tipped over to spill slowly down her cheek.

'I tried so hard not to love you again.' It was time to say it all…from the heart. 'I never stopped,' she managed shakily. 'Even when I hated you.' She traced his cheek with gentle fingers. 'You're the love of my life,' she said simply. 'My heart, my soul…they're yours. Always.'

'*Dios mediante,*' Xavier added softly. 'You have my word I'll never give you cause to regret it.'

A slight movement of her hand sent brilliant prisms of red and blue fire from the ring he'd gifted her. She had nothing that came close in value to give him in return…except one thing. Symbolic, she mused, but infinitely precious.

'Stay there.'

'*Amada,*' he assured her gently. 'I'm not going anywhere.'

The breath caught in his throat as her mouth curved into a sparkling smile, and he had to tamp down the urge to take possession of her in a manner that would leave no room for doubt.

Instead, he released her and watched as she disappeared into the *en suite,* only to re-emerge less than a minute later and hand him a small rectangular packet.

'For you.' To alleviate any doubt, she added, 'I've no further need to take them.'

The significance didn't escape him, and she met his careful scrutiny with equanimity. 'It's all I have to give you,' she said simply.

'Everything you are,' he responded gently. 'Is all I could ever want.'

'A child...children. *Ours,*' she added softly. 'Will complete the joy we share. Don't you think?'

She undid him. Always would, he perceived, as he drew her close and closed his mouth over her own.

All the actions he'd taken, every path he'd traversed in life...had led to this woman.

Without her, he'd merely exist as an empty, emotionless shell. And he proceeded to tell her, with such deep sensitivity, it almost brought her to tears.

When he was done, she pressed light fingers to his mouth and gave him a smile to die for. 'Just for the record, could you translate that into English?'

He did, catching the slow spill of tears as she failed to still their fall.

'Time, I think,' Xavier uttered quietly, 'to indulge in distraction.'

'What do you have in mind?'

He reached for the zip fastening on her wedding gown, and slowly freed it, removing each layer until she stood naked before him.

All she'd been able to manage was his jacket and tie and to free the buttons on his shirt, and he easily divested what remained, then he drew her down onto the bed.

Their lovemaking became something incredibly special… a sensual tasting that led to a conflagration of the senses. Tactile, spiritual, emotional.

Electrifying passion at its zenith, merging two souls, two hearts as one.

An intrinsic knowledge they belonged together for all time…and beyond.

* * * * *

*Harlequin Intrigue top author Delores Fossen presents
a brand-new series of breathtaking romantic suspense!*
TEXAS MATERNITY: HOSTAGES
The first installment available May 2010:
THE BABY'S GUARDIAN

Shaw cursed and hooked his arm around Sabrina.

Despite the urgency that the deadly gunfire created, he tried to be careful with her, and he took the brunt of the fall when he pulled her to the ground. His shoulder hit hard, but he held on tight to his gun so that it wouldn't be jarred from his hand.

Shaw didn't stop there. He crawled over Sabrina, sheltering her pregnant belly with his body, and he came up ready to return fire.

This was obviously a situation he'd wanted to avoid at all cost. He didn't want his baby in the middle of a fight with these armed fugitives, but when they fired that shot, they'd left him no choice. Now, the trick was to get Sabrina safely out of there.

"Get down," someone on the SWAT team yelled from the roof of the adjacent building.

Shaw did. He dropped lower, covering Sabrina as best he could.

There was another shot, but this one came from a rifleman on the SWAT team. Shaw didn't look up, but he heard the sound of glass being blown apart.

The shots continued, all coming from his men, which meant it might be time to try to get Sabrina to better cover. Shaw glanced at the front of the building.

So that Sabrina's pregnant belly wouldn't be smashed against the ground, Shaw eased off her and moved her to a sitting position so that her back was against the brick wall. They were close. Too close. And face-to-face.

He found himself staring right into those sea-green eyes.

How will Shaw get Sabrina out?
Follow the daring rescue and the heartbreaking
aftermath in THE BABY'S GUARDIAN
by Delores Fossen,
available May 2010 from Harlequin Intrigue.

Bestselling Harlequin Presents® author

Lynne Graham

introduces

VIRGIN ON HER WEDDING NIGHT

Valente Lorenzatto never forgave Caroline Hales's
abandonment of him at the altar. But now he's
made millions and claimed his aristocratic Venetian
birthright—and he's poised to get his revenge.
He'll ruin Caroline's family by buying out their
company and throwing them out of their mansion...
unless she agrees to give him the wedding night
she denied him five years ago....

**Available May 2010
from Harlequin Presents!**

HARLEQUIN® *Blaze*™

is proud to introduce...

New York Times bestselling author

Brenda Jackson

with
SPONTANEOUS

Kim Cannon and Duan Jeffries have a great thing going.
Whenever they meet up, the passion between them
is hot, intense...spontaneous. And things really heat
up when Duan agrees to accompany her to her
mother's wedding. Too bad there's something
he's not telling her....

Don't miss the fireworks!

*Available in May 2010
wherever Harlequin Blaze books are sold.*

red-hot reads

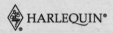
HARLEQUIN®

INTRIGUE®

HARLEQUIN INTRIGUE® AUTHOR**

DELORES FOSSEN

**PRESENTS AN ALL-NEW
THRILLING TRILOGY**

TEXAS MATERNITY: HOSTAGES

When masked gunmen take over the maternity ward at a San Antonio hospital, local cops, FBI and the scared mothers can't figure out any possible motive. Before long, secrets are revealed, and a city that has been on edge since the siege began learns the truth behind the negotiations and must deal with the fallout.

LOOK FOR

THE BABY'S GUARDIAN, *May*
DEVASTATING DADDY, *June*
THE MOMMY MYSTERY, *July*

www.eHarlequin.com HI69472

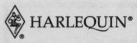
HARLEQUIN®

American ★ Romance®

LAURA MARIE ALTOM

The Baby Twins

Stephanie Olmstead has her hands full raising
her twin baby girls on her own. When she runs
into old friend Brady Flynn, she's shocked to find
herself suddenly attracted to the handsome airline
pilot! Will this flyboy be the perfect daddy—
or will he crash and burn?

Babies
&
Bachelors
USA

"LOVE, HOME & HAPPINESS"

www.eHarlequin.com

HAR75309

HARLEQUIN
Ambassadors

Want to share your passion for reading Harlequin® Books?

Become a Harlequin Ambassador!

Harlequin Ambassadors are a group of passionate and well-connected readers who are willing to share their joy of reading Harlequin® books with family and friends.

You'll be sent all the tools you need to spark great conversation, including free books!

All we ask is that you share the romance with your friends and family!

You'll also be invited to have a say in new book ideas and exchange opinions with women just like you!

To see if you qualify* to be a Harlequin Ambassador, please visit www.HarlequinAmbassadors.com.

Thank you for your participation.

BAP098PA

REQUEST YOUR FREE BOOKS!

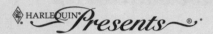

2 FREE NOVELS PLUS
2 FREE GIFTS!

YES! Please send me 2 FREE Harlequin Presents® novels and my 2 FREE gifts (gifts are worth about $10). After receiving them, if I don't wish to receive any more books, I can return the shipping statement marked "cancel." If I don't cancel, I will receive 6 brand-new novels every month and be billed just $4.05 per book in the U.S. or $4.74 per book in Canada. That's a saving of close to 15% off the cover price! It's quite a bargain! Shipping and handling is just 50¢ per book in the U.S. and 75¢ per book in Canada.* I understand that accepting the 2 free books and gifts places me under no obligation to buy anything. I can always return a shipment and cancel at any time. Even if I never buy another book, the two free books and gifts are mine to keep forever.

106 HDN E4FN 306 HDN E4FY

Name	(PLEASE PRINT)	
Address		Apt. #
City	State/Prov.	Zip/Postal Code

Signature (if under 18, a parent or guardian must sign)

Mail to the **Harlequin Reader Service:**
IN U.S.A.: P.O. Box 1867, Buffalo, NY 14240-1867
IN CANADA: P.O. Box 609, Fort Erie, Ontario L2A 5X3

Not valid for current subscribers to Harlequin Presents books.

Are you a current subscriber to Harlequin Presents books and want to receive the larger-print edition? Call 1-800-873-8635 today!

* Terms and prices subject to change without notice. Prices do not include applicable taxes. N.Y. residents add applicable sales tax. Canadian residents will be charged applicable provincial taxes and GST. Offer not valid in Quebec. This offer is limited to one order per household. All orders subject to approval. Credit or debit balances in a customer's account(s) may be offset by any other outstanding balance owed by or to the customer. Please allow 4 to 6 weeks for delivery. Offer available while quantities last.

Former bad boy Sloan Hawkins is back in Redemption, Oklahoma, to help keep his aunt's cherished garden thriving and to reconnect with the girl he left behind, Annie Markham. But when he discovers his secret child—and that single mother Annie never stopped loving him—he's determined that a wedding will take place in the garden nurtured by faith and love.

REDEMPTION
RIVER

Where healing flows...

Look for

The Wedding Garden

by Linda Goodnight

*Available May 2010
wherever you buy books.*

www.SteepleHill.com

Steeple
Hill®

LI87595

HARLEQUIN Presents

Coming Next Month

in **Harlequin Presents® EXTRA.** Available April 13, 2010.

#97 RICH, RUTHLESS AND SECRETLY ROYAL
Robyn Donald
Regally Wed

#98 FORGOTTEN MISTRESS, SECRET LOVE-CHILD
Annie West
Regally Wed

#99 TAKEN BY THE PIRATE TYCOON
Daphne Clair
Ruthless Tycoons

#100 ITALIAN MARRIAGE: IN NAME ONLY
Kathryn Ross
Ruthless Tycoons

Coming Next Month

in **Harlequin Presents®.** Available April 27, 2010:

#2915 VIRGIN ON HER WEDDING NIGHT
Lynne Graham

#2916 TAMED: THE BARBARIAN KING
Jennie Lucas
Dark-Hearted Desert Men

#2917 BLACKWOLF'S REDEMPTION
Sandra Marton
Men Without Mercy

#2918 THE PRINCE'S CHAMBERMAID
Sharon Kendrick
At His Service

#2919 MISTRESS: PREGNANT BY THE SPANISH BILLIONAIRE
Kim Lawrence

#2920 RUTHLESS RUSSIAN, LOST INNOCENCE
Chantelle Shaw